NEVER CATCH THE BOUQUET

RIVER LAURENT

Never Catch The Bouquet

978-1-911608-29-5

AUTHOR'S NOTE

With love
for every girl who never caught the bouquet.

CHAPTER 1

ANNETTE

"Can't believe she's really married now," Gia murmured, shaking her head.

"Me neither," I agreed, taking a sip of cold champagne and gazing at Collette.

She looked beautiful against the backdrop of the gorgeous hotel garden that they'd hired for the wedding reception. And it was patently clear that the bride and groom were perfectly suited to one another. Collette met Andrew in college, and the two of them have been head-over-heels in love ever since. To be honest we were all surprised it'd taken them this long to tie the knot, but they wanted to do it right: a fabulous weekend party in Vegas, all their friends and family around them.

I turned my gaze back to Gia. "Looks like I'm the only one out of the three of us left on the shelf."

"Oh, come on." Gia chuckled and waved her hand, making the diamond in her wedding ring catch the noon sun's rays and almost blind me. "It's not a race."

"Spoken like someone who's way out in front already," I pointed out.

"Don't be so silly, Annette. There's no rush. You've still got all the time in the world to meet someone. She paused and frowned. "You're not worried, are you?"

Gia had Nathan, a whirlwind romance that had ended in a marriage after just six months. Collette had Andrew. And I had…I had nobody. Nobody at all. My shoulders wanted to slump, but I turned it into a careless shrug. "No, of course not. I never think about it. It's just today, you know."

"Good, because it's only a matter of time before some lucky guy comes to claim you. You're gorgeous."

"I am?" I muttered. I certainly didn't feel it in my soft-lemon colored bridesmaid's dress. Somehow, Gia managed to carry it off, but I actually felt quite fat and unattractive.

"Collette, it's time to toss the bouquet," Francine, the wedding planner announced. She'd been holding the whole event together with mind-bogglingly impressive efficiency.

I'd already made a note to get her number…not for me, of course, but in case one of the girls at work needed it.

Collette, clutching her bouquet of beautiful flowers to her chest, whirled around, and beamed at me.

I started to shake my head, but she was waggling her eyebrows so vigorously she was in danger of dislodging her tiara.

"No," I mouthed in a panic.

"Yes," she mouthed back happily. She hadn't been able to wipe the smile off her face all day.

I couldn't have been happier for her, especially when I'd stood beside her as she swore herself to Andrew forever, but there was no way she was throwing that damn bouquet at me.

A crowd began to gather around Collette to watch her toss the bouquet. A gaggle of single women had come out of the woodwork to catch it too, which was a good thing because I was out of here. The last thing I wanted to do was expose myself as a desperate husband hunter, so I took a step back.

Gia's hand closed tightly over my wrist. "Don't you dare," she muttered while displaying all her whitened teeth in big smile.

"Ready?" Collette called, as she glanced around and shot a look directly at me.

I wanted to wave my hands and beg her not to aim it in my direction, but once Collette makes her mind up….

"Here we go!" she shouted as the bouquet looped through the air towards me. A cheer went up from the crowd as Gia released my wrist and grabbed my champagne glass from my other hand. I could have sworn time slowed down as the flash of color headed in my direction. Women around me stood motionless with mouths agape. Only one or two rushed to where I was. Suddenly, I forgot I didn't want to appear undignified or desperate.

All I knew was I had to catch that damn bouquet.

No matter what.

CHAPTER 2

ANNETTE

I planted my feet into the ground, bent my knees like a quarterback, and jumped into the air with both my hands outstretched and clawed. Adrenaline flowed in my veins. This bouquet was mine. I could already smell the scent of its flowers in my nostrils.

As my hands began to close on it, a great big bear of a dog, leapt up out of nowhere and crashed into me, knocking me to the ground. I could only watch in disbelief as he sailed on by and snatched the bouquet right out of the air.

At first, the crowd gasped in shock to see me land flat on my back on the lovely grass, but then they chuckled nervously when I instantly sprung up to my feet like a rubber ball and even though my face was bright red with humiliation, I pretended as if I wasn't absolutely mortified and humiliated, and said with a casual laugh, "Well, that decided that. Next one to the altar is the big hairy dog."

No doubt, my dress had a large grass stain running all the

way down the back. The shock was wearing away as I could feel the muscles of my thighs and buttocks start to throb.

"Annette!" Collette gasped, running towards me. "Are you all right?"

"I'm fine," I replied, trying to laugh it off. I felt like such an idiot. "What I want to know is who invited that big hairy thing to your wedding?"

"Here, let me give you a hand," Gia said, as she surreptitiously tried to wipe away whatever stains were on my butt.

Collette's wedding planner arrived at Collette's side. She gave me a fake smile. "Never mind. You'll catch it next time."

I smiled at her through gritted teeth.

"Now, if you don't mind, I need to borrow the bride," she murmured, gently slipping her hand over the small of Collette's back.

"I'm sorry, Annette," Collette called as she was being guided away.

I grinned. "Don't worry. Go. It's your big day."

Gia patted my shoulder. "You're not hurt, are you?"

I ignored the throbbing in my muscles and shook my head. "Just my dignity." I let my gaze swing away from Gia and spotted my grandmother, Hazel, bustling towards me through the crowd. It opened up in front of her, like she was Moses parting the sea.

"Annette, darling," she called.

I waved at her as she approached.

"I'll give you two a minute," Gia murmured, ducking off in the direction of the drinks table.

I smiled as my grandmother gave me a quick hug and looked me up and down.

"You don't look hurt," she remarked confidently.

I laughed. "Yeah, I'm fine." I waved my hand. "Just a tangle, that's all."

"Shame you couldn't have caught that bouquet. Silly dog. Who brings dogs to weddings, anyway? That bouquet had your name on it." She sniffed dramatically.

I fought the urge to roll my eyes at her. "It doesn't guarantee anything, Nana. I'm not going to meet the man of my dreams just because I catch the bouquet. It's just a superstition."

"I know, I know." She gestured with her hands in that way she did when she was letting me know she wasn't interested carrying on with a conversation any longer.

I knew every little one of her tics by now; she raised me, after all, when at the age of six my parents and both my younger brothers were killed in a car accident. My maternal grandmother lived in England and we were not close so basically, I knew no other family than Nana. She was always the one I turned to for advice.

Sure, she could be a little old-fashioned sometimes, but that was just her way and I didn't hold it against her. She was of a different generation to me and in her world, not being married off at thirty was basically embracing a life of spinsterhood. Every conversation we've had recently seemed aimed at figuring out when I was going to settle down and give her the grandkids she was so desperate for.

"But with *both* Gia and Collette married now…" She let her sentence drift away. Collette and Gia had been my friends for years and she saw them almost as much as her own as she did me.

"Yeah, I know." I glanced around. "But there's no rush, is there? It's just something to look forward to when the right guy comes along."

She fell silent, her eyes downcast, and her mouth suddenly trembling.

I stared at her. "Nana?" I prompted. "What's wrong?"

She looked up at me, and I could tell that she was keeping something from me. We didn't have secrets from one another. You didn't grow up in such close contact with someone and get to keep anything from them. The first day I brought home a packet of condoms she found them in my jeans pocket.

"There is some rush," she replied quietly….so quietly that the words were almost absorbed by the buzz of the crowd around us.

"What are you talking about?" I took her hand and squeezed it gently.

"I'm…not well, baby."

"What do you mean?" I prompted. I felt as though the ground was shifting out from beneath my feet.

"I don't have long left to live," she admitted.

A cold wash of panic jolted through me. "What are you talking about?"

She shook her head. "I'm sorry, baby."

"Nana, what the hell is going on?"

She bit her bottom lip and looked at me as if she pitied me.

Suddenly, I got it. It was a joke. One of Nana's not so funny, little pranks. She must be joking. There was no way this could be real. "Very funny, Nana, but I'm not playing along with this one. If it had been anything else but your health I would have."

She shook her head sadly and even looked a little hurt by my words. "I would never joke about something like this."

I realized at once that she must be telling the truth. Part of me wanted to grab her and shake her to get her to admit that all of this was nothing more than a sick, twisted-up joke she was playing on me, but I knew she would never have said anything like this as a gag. She was telling the truth. After what had happened with my parents and brothers, surely, she would never wisecrack about something as serious as this. I had only thought this because I felt too shocked and I simply didn't want to believe she was that ill.

I swallowed hard. I couldn't make a scene here, not at my best friend's wedding. I needed to keep myself together. I just had no clue how in the name of holy hell I was meant to do that in the face of what she was telling me. "What's wrong with you?" I whispered.

"Let's not discuss the gory details now. I just want to see you happy with someone." She looked up at me, her eyes glistening with tears. "I want to know that you'll be taken care of after I'm gone."

8

"Please, don't talk like that," I begged her, my voice breaking. I could already feel tears burning at the backs of my eyes.

"Honey, I don't know how long I have and I need to know that someone's going to be there for you when I'm gone. That someone's going to be your family..." She glanced away from me, tilting her gaze towards the ground.

I tried to make sense of what she was telling me. The only real family I had left in the world was about to blink out of it. And I would be all alone once more.

"Annette," Collette called from behind me.

I had to force myself back into party-guest mode. I couldn't let her see me upset. This was meant to be her day, and I wasn't going to undercut it with anything happening in my life. I knew she loved my nana as much as I did, and she would be devastated if she heard the truth.

"Are you all right?" She slowed her pace as she came to join me. "Did you get hurt when the dog knocked you over?"

"No, no, I'm fine." I forced a smile. "Don't worry about me, really."

"I've told Francine I want to throw the bouquet again," she said gently.

For a moment, I felt as though I might just burst into tears right there in front of her. I had to get out of here before I exploded with emotion. Part of me felt numb and part of me felt like I would scream so loud the entire party would grind to a halt.

"Annette?" Collette called worriedly.

"You were going to the bathroom, weren't you, dear?" Nana

remarked, widening her eyes at me, clearly sensing how close I was to the edge, silently urging me out of here quickly.

I nodded. "That's right. I'm off to the Ladies. You go and party with everyone else. Don't worry about me. Throw the bouquet again if you want, but I want nothing to do with it, okay? We both know I never catch the bouquet. I didn't catch the bouquet at Gia's wedding and I didn't catch yours."

Collette gave me a long look. "Are you sure?"

I plastered a smile on my face and patted her arm. "I'm very sure."

"All right," she said slowly before heading back to join her new husband and the rest of her guests on their carefree evening together.

I watched as she went, and then turned to Nana.

"You need to go get some privacy, child," she ordered firmly.

Even in light of what she'd just told me, I knew arguing with her wouldn't end well. It rarely did. She knew all of my tricks and even after years working in a law office, I wasn't sure there would be much I could have done to get around her.

CHAPTER 3

ANNETTE

I hurried off to the bathroom, and just made it into one of the stalls before I started freaking out properly. I was hyperventilating. My brain felt as though it would explode. All of this had to be some sort of awful joke. This day was meant to be joyous, happy, something we could look back on and smile about. But now it would be inextricably linked with the horrible knowledge of me being so close to losing the one family member I still had left.

None of this was fair. None of it. I felt as though my entire life I had been fighting an uphill battle towards something that resembled happiness. I knew no one was owed anything, certainly not happiness, security or comfort, but I'd worked *so hard* to try and secure those things for myself and the people I cared about. Now the universe just looked down at all my efforts and spat on them. I couldn't believe this was real.

I put my head between my knees and tried to catch my breath. I felt sure that any moment now, someone would come in and tell me I was being pranked. Then I would be mad and upset at the fact anyone would think this was funny, but I would get over it, because none of it mattered as long as my precious Nana was sticking around with me. I knew she was old, knew she hadn't been doing so great lately, but I'd assumed she would shake it off.

Not succumb to it.

God, I wanted to scream. I wanted to storm out there to everyone having a good time and tell them they had to stop at once, because no one could be happy in the face of what my beautiful grandmother was going through. In what world was this all right? In what world was this okay? Everything she'd done for me for the last thirty years of my life. I'd been saving for years to take her on a big all expenses paid trip through Asia, staying at the best hotels. All those countries she'd always wanted to visit. She wasn't going anywhere.

And there was nothing I could do to stop it.

I thought back to the bouquet and wondered if she was right. Maybe I needed someone, someone other than my friends, a real partner who could stand by my side when things got hard. Maybe that support was something I would need going forward from this. A family, a real family, one of my own. Had I been so focused on work all this time that I had neglected to focus on what really mattered? I had taken my nana for granted, assumed she would just always be there for me when I needed her. Now, a stark reminder of the fact that she wouldn't had just come crashing down on my head, and I couldn't hide from it any longer.

I lifted my head and tried to catch my breath. My make-up was probably ruined, but I didn't care. I couldn't imagine walking out there and putting a game face on, pretending I felt anything other than utter and complete emptiness.

Eventually, a couple of women bustled into the bathroom, chatting excitedly.

"Oh, and did you see Cole?" one of them asked the other.

I lurked behind the door. I knew exactly who they were talking about. Cole Newman, Collette's drop-dead gorgeous older brother. He was the most talked-about member of that family.

"How could I possibly miss him?" The other woman sighed as she washed her hands.

"I'm pretty sure he was checking me out during the ceremony. Did you see him do that?"

"I think he was checking out anyone he could get his eyes on," her friend replied, sounding slightly exhausted by the conversation.

"Don't be such a cynic," woman one shot back.

"I'm only a cynic because I actually *listen* to what people say about him."

"Yeah, well, you can't trust gossip—"

"It's not gossip if it's literally all anyone talks about when it comes to him," woman two cut her off.

Despite myself, I almost snorted with laughter. She was right. Cole had more than a reputation. There were about three women left in the tri-state area he hadn't hooked up with. Gia and I were two of those three. He had some peculiar draw over women. As matter of fact, I would have been lying if I said I didn't get it at least somewhat. With a crop of dark hair that only the exceptionally gorgeous could pull off, he had a slightly crooked smile and sexy chocolate brown eyes that seemed like hot pools that you could drown in. Not that I had spent too long looking into them.

"Well, I still think I'm in with a chance," the first woman insisted. "And apparently he's amazing in—"

Before they could continue, I shot to my feet, pushed the door open and stepped out. I really didn't want to hear what they had to say about my best friend's big brother's performance in the sack, thank you very much.

They both glanced at me, then turned their attention back to the mirrors, clearly wondering how much of their conversation I had heard.

I washed my hands and checked my make-up. It wasn't as bad as I'd thought it would be, but my face looked drawn, shocked. I knew if I walked back out into the party looking like this, people would guess at once something was wrong. In some selfish part of my brain, I wished Nana had waited to tell me, at least until I could have had a little time to figure everything out.

Laughing about something, the women left.

I had to pull myself together if I didn't want to wind up ruining my best friend's wedding. Splashing my face with water, I fixed my hair. Taking a deep breath, I prepared myself to head back out there. I had to make it through today, and then I could focus on what the hell I would do with Nana.

I headed out of the door, eyes fixed to the ground, and before

I could get too far, I crashed straight into someone. "Oh, sorry—" I started to apologize, but before I could get out anything of meaning, I found myself staring into the deep brown eyes of the devil himself.

"Hey, Annette," he greeted, his strong hands curling around my upper-arms.

"Hey, Cole." What were the chances I would run into him right after hearing those women talking about him?

"Hey, are you all right?" he asked, furrowing his brow and taking my shoulders in his strong hands.

The sudden physical contact, the care in his eyes, was all I needed to push me over the edge. I felt my face crumple. All the emotions I had been trying my best to keep in leaked out of me before I had a chance to get myself in hand.

"What's wrong?" he asked, quickly putting his arm around me and leading me away from the bathrooms towards a quieter part of the hotel.

I barely knew this man. We had met at a few pre-wedding functions and I'd run into him around Collette's place a few times, but that had been it. The most I knew about him was his reputation, but nothing else. So why was I letting this guy see the most vulnerable parts of myself? "I'm sorry." I shook my head and tried to catch my breath, but the tears were coming fast and hard by now. "I just had some hard news and—"

"Let's get you away from here," he suggested, glancing over his shoulder at the party behind us. "I could use some air as well."

15

"My room's upstairs," I told him, trying to wipe away the tears streaming down my cheeks.

I told him the number and he quickly led me into the elevator, away from everyone else. I guess I just felt so grateful for someone else taking control as the thought of trying to keep my shit together in front of those people out there was nearly impossible.

I fished my key from my purse and let us inside. As soon as the door was shut behind me, I crashed on the bed and curled into a ball.

"Are you okay? Do you need me to get you something?" he asked, taking off the expensive blazer he was wearing and rolling up the sleeves of his shirt.

"No, no." I shook my head and pushed myself up. "I'm sorry. I shouldn't have dragged you all the way up here. Thanks for bringing me up here, but I'm all right now. Go down to the party, you shouldn't miss it because of me."

"Look, my sister wants this day to be perfect for everyone," he remarked firmly. "And she's going to be pissed if she knows that I left one of her bridesmaids up here crying."

"Fine." I sighed and pointed to the minibar. "Get me a drink?"

"What's your poison?"

"Anything," I replied.

He grabbed two tiny bottles of whiskey. They were so tiny they disappeared into his fists.

I paused. "Hang on. I've been on champagne all day if I drink that I'll be saddled with a headache I don't need tomorrow. Just open the bottle of champagne in the fridge."

His eyebrows rose, but he made short work of popping the cork and pouring it into two flutes. He handed me one.

"Should we drink to something?" I asked.

"To us," he said with a smile.

"That's good enough for me." I sank back into the pillows on the bed and took a long draw. It was good to be near someone right now, even if it was someone I barely knew.

"So, what's going on?" he asked softly, lifting the glass up to his lips.

"It's my grandmother." I rubbed my hand over my face. "She just told me—she's sick."

"Hmm…How sick?"

"Like, she's counting down the months or maybe even weeks, sick," I replied miserably, unable to believe these particular words were really coming out of my mouth.

He winced. "I'm so sorry," he replied gently.

His voice was so sweet and kind I nearly burst into tears again, but I forced myself to keep it together. Instead, I drained the glass and held it out.

He refilled it silently. "Is she here?"

I nodded.

He got to his feet, towering over me. "You want me to go get her for you?"

"No. I don't know if I can bear to see her without breaking down right now," I confessed, shaking my head. "I don't want to ruin this day for everyone else. Which I'm aware I'm in the middle of doing for you right now, by the way."

"You're not ruining anything," he assured me, his mouth curling upwards.

Even in my state, I recognized it as a very attractive thing. A sexy thing. "That's sweet of you to say," I murmured.

"Not sweet, true," he replied suavely.

I took another sip of my champagne. I suddenly felt quite drunk. How much had I been drinking today? Since this morning when we toasted the bride. This might have been a bad idea. I should send him away. I don't want to get into any situation I would definitely regret. This was Collette's older brother, for God's sake. "Anyway, if you want to leave…"

"I don't," he said softly.

I cleared my throat. Okay, let him just finish his drink. Then he can go. It would be rude of me to just throw him out when he'd been kind enough to bring me up here. "This is weird."

"What is?"

"I don't know. Having you up here in my room. Alone."

He smiled. "Just relax, okay? You're my little sister's best friend. I'm not going to jump you."

I flushed scarlet. "I didn't mean to be rude or anything. I know I'm obviously not your type."

Something flashed in his eyes. "How do you know what's my type?"

I choked on my champagne spluttering and gasping for breath.

He came forward, gently took the glass out of my hand, and stood over me while I endured my embarrassing coughing fit.

Was it not bad enough that I fell in front of everyone, now I've had to go and humiliate myself in front of Cole Newman?

He handed me some tissues.

I plucked them from his hands, wiped my eyes, and held them to my burning face. "I'm sorry. I just meant you only go out with beautiful girls."

"You are beautiful. Very beautiful."

My head jerked up in astonishment.

He stared down at me, a frown appearing on his forehead. "Surely, you must know that."

Confused, I looked into the utterly captivating eyes of my unlikely savior. A playboy who probably had a dozen women waiting for him impatiently downstairs. "Oh god, I really don't know what I'm meant to do, anymore."

"You don't have to do anything right now…except finish your drink," he said.

I swear, I wanted to stop being a responsible adult and just drown in those warm chocolate pools of sheer decadence.

CHAPTER 4

COLE

One of my sister's best friends sat on a bed in front of me. The last time this kind of thing happened, I was seventeen. I shot out of there like a bat out of hell and ever since I'd avoided all her starry-eyed friends like the fucking plague. But it didn't feel awkward with Annette. Probably because she looked so sad, like someone had dropped her from a great height and broken her. Strangely, I wanted nothing more than to pull her into my arms and tell her everything would be okay, but it would have been a lie.

"Thank you for doing this." She looked up at me ruefully. Her make-up a little smudged, and her dress hiked up, revealing a wedge of smooth thigh.

"Oh, come on." I waved my hand dismissively. "I should be thanking you for saving me. Down there, it was all fake smiles and flirting."

"I thought that was kind of your thing?"

"What are you saying?"

She cocked an eyebrow at me. "I've heard about your reputation," she replied tartly. "I think everyone in this place has."

"What reputation?" I asked, even though I knew exactly what she was talking about. I'd been a rogue when I was younger, but not anymore. Been there done that. At the end of the day, it ended up being a temporary, shallow business. All those bodies and I had nothing to show for it.

"Oh, just the reputation that you're the biggest lady killer in the state."

I chuckled. "Don't you think that might be a bit of an exaggeration—"

"Are you kidding me?" she cut me off. "I heard a couple of girls in the bathroom talking about you. Trust me, people know who you are."

"I don't know if that's a good thing or not," I admitted. As a younger man, I might have been proud to know I had a reputation of that nature, pleased to see I had made my mark on the women of my social circle. But now being older, maybe that reputation wasn't going so good for me after all. When people looked at me, they saw a player.

"Trust me, better to have the reputation of a playboy," she replied glumly. "Than be the woman who lost out to the big hairy dog."

I smiled. "I don't know about you, but if I were to lose out to anyone I'd rather it was to a big hairy dog."

"Did I look really ridiculous?"

Ridiculous? She was beautiful. I noticed this as soon as I laid eyes on her, passing through Collette's apartment one evening in the city. Curvy, with thick auburn hair and the greenest eyes I'd ever seen in my life. She'd caught my eye at once, but I knew better than to go after any of Collette's friends, so I hadn't pursued things any further.

"Actually, don't answer that. Of course, I looked ridiculous."

"Actually, I thought you looked rather…heroic."

She glanced down at her bridesmaid dress. "Now, you're just buttering me up. I doubt anyone could look heroic in this frilly disaster."

"You did," I told her honestly.

For second, she stared at me suspiciously.

I stared right back. I wasn't lying. Then, without warning, the air in the room changed, it became thick with something different. I finished off the champagne I had liberated from the minibar and placed the glass on the table.

Her eyes slid away from mine as she laughed nervously. "Anyway, I shouldn't keep you here any longer. There must be dozens of girls waiting for you."

"Is this a competition? Do you want me to tell you about the dozens of guys who would be jealous if they knew I was in your room with you?"

"Dozens of guys, huh?" she repeated breathlessly.

"Dozens," I echoed.

Before I had a chance to say anything more, she leaned forward and planted a kiss on my lips.

When I'd brought her up here, my thoughts had been about as far removed from sex, as they could possibly be. But as soon as our lips met, I felt an almost feral surge of attraction to her... so strong it shocked me. I wanted to fuck my sister's best friend! I should stop right now. This was my last chance, but I couldn't. It was like asking a kid not to open his Christmas presents while everyone else was opening theirs. I sank down on to the bed next to her.

Thank God, I'd thought to bring a packet of condoms along to this thing. Even though I hadn't come with anyone in mind, a family wedding usually meant I would probably wind up sleeping with someone. Even if the woman currently making out with me was about the last one, I'd imagined it would actually be with.

She pulled back, looked away, and shook her head. "I'm really sorry," she whispered. "I don't know what the hell I was thinking."

"It's fine." I brushed a strand of hair from her face. My eyes locked on her mouth. When she bit her plump bottom lip, hot blood rushed to my cock. I wanted to rip her dress off her. "No matter what the circumstances, isn't it right for a groomsman and a bridesmaid to hook up at the wedding?"

"I just needed something to get my mind off of this thing with Nana," she mumbled, her eyes enormous and her cheeks pink.

"I'm happy to help. If you want it, you can have it. You just have to ask for it."

Her breath caught and one word trembled out. "Cole."

The effect was startling. It felt like she'd called to my soul. My heart began to beat hard and fast while my skin tingled with static electricity the way it did before a big storm. I knew I was doing something I shouldn't, fooling around with one of my sister's best friends, but I wanted her and she wanted to get her mind off whatever she was going through, and if we could both find some mutual pleasure in this, then…what was the harm?

I traced my finger down her neck and watched her shiver. She stayed as still as a stone when I leaned towards her, but when I pressed my lips against hers she moaned helplessly against my mouth. I slipped my tongue inside, tasting her, the sharpness and the sweetness of the champagne mixed with something individually and utterly *her*. I could already feel myself rock hard and ready to burst. I moved my hands over her body and guided her down onto the bed, running my fingers up along the smooth flesh of her deliciously thick thighs. Her eyes never left mine when I lifted the hem of her dress and exposed her panties. Ah, white cotton. How sweet.

"Open your legs, Annette."

Licking her lips, she parted her smooth thighs.

I cupped my hand around her mound, over her panties, feeling the warmth of her core through the fabric. She pushed herself up towards me, letting out a groan of need as she ground her pussy against my hand, and I knew neither of us would be able to hold on much longer.

As I bent my head and kissed her deeply she moved her hand down between my legs and gripped my cock, squeezing gently.

I ran butterfly kisses down her neck, over her throat, guiding down the straps of the dress so I could brush my mouth over her shoulders. Sliding my finger under her panties, I found her clit and stroked it gently, feeling her wetness as it spread over my fingers.

"Oh…" She groaned, pressing her head into my shoulders.

I moved further down with my mouth, peeling the dress down so I could suck on her nipples gently. She tasted so good. Clean skin and something else even more tempting. It made me desperate to taste her pussy.

I could have feasted on her all day long, but I wanted to go further. Slipping down between her legs, I pushed her legs apart as far as they would go and pressed my mouth on her pussy through her panties and breathed hot air into her. She arched her back from the bed and groaned. I could smell her muskiness through the fabric of the white cotton of her underwear. She reached for my head, running her fingers through my hair, as I swiftly stripped her down, tossed her panties aside, and leaned back to look at her pink little pussy for the first time.

"Damn," I muttered under my breath.

She was glistening with wetness, rocking her hips back and forth with need in front of me. I had gone down on plenty of women in the past, but something about seeing what lay between her thighs flicked a switch in my brain I didn't even realize had been there until this moment. All this time I secretly lusted after Collette's friend. I wanted nothing more than to plunge forward, draw her into my mouth and fill myself with her until there was room for nothing more. In the dim light of the hotel room, she looked like the sweetest thing in the world.

I wouldn't deny myself a taste any longer.

I leaned forward and brushed my mouth over her, just softly, feeling out the way her body responded to my touch. The way her thighs clenched beneath my hands and she let out a long breath, as though flushing something from her system. I ran my tongue up and down her slit.

Fuck, she tasted incredible, sweet and addictive.

Her hands gripped the bed linen when I sealed my lips around her clit, and began to suck lightly, gently, teasing her with my tongue. As I did so, I knew I would have a hard time forgetting about this. I'd been through so many encounters with so many different women that they had started to blur together in my mind, but this was something else, something else entirely. Who knew why, but the details of this encounter were already burned onto my brain for good.

I grabbed her ass and lavished her pussy with attention, sucking, licking, and tending to her every way she would let me. She grasped my head and held me in place, grinding up against me hungrily, her body moving in time with mine. With my face buried in her sweet pussy, I slipped a thick finger inside of her tight wetness. She flexed around me uncontrollably, and I knew she couldn't take much more. She would come in my mouth at any moment.

"Cole," she screamed, as her entire body jerked and shook.

She came hard. Not holding back. Not being coy, just letting it all out. Raw, animal, wild. And it was just beautiful. I hungrily licked the juices that run down her thighs possessively.

As if she were mine.

Which was weird, because of course, she wasn't mine. We were just having fun.

As if she read my mind, she reached down, pulled me up on top of her, and kissed me hungrily as if she wanted to mark my soul with her kiss. I could taste the mix of her pussy and her lips on my tongue. "Now fuck me," she breathed in my ear.

I didn't need telling twice. My cock was painfully rigid with need.

I reached into my pocket for a condom. "Keep your legs wide open," I growled as I pulled down my pants, my underwear and sheathed myself quickly. She was dripping with desire and it turned me on to see the thick cream that oozed out as her body prepared itself for my cock.

"Jesus, you're big," she breathed, her eyes widening.

She slid her hands over my shoulders while she waited to take me inside of her. With the taste of her pussy still fresh on my lips, I positioned my cock head at her entrance. I could feel her hot opening begging for my cock.

She closed her eyes to savor the sensation of my cock penetrating her. "Oh, my God," she gasped when her little lips spread out on either side of my cock and my shaft pushed into her tight heat.

She leaned up to kiss me once more; it was as though every moment her lips weren't on mine she was hurting for them. I knew how she felt. There was a strange depth of connection here, something beyond the normal one-night-stand.

I grabbed her hips. "Easy," I warned. If she moved too fast, I wouldn't be able to control myself. I wrapped my arms around her and drew her in close to me as I thrust into her, moving slow, taking my time. I wanted this to last. I wanted this to go on as long as it possibly could.

My cock slid all the way in. I loved the way her pussy took all of me.

"Oh, Cole. You feel so damn good," she whispered. "So damn good."

I wasn't sure how long we were going at it like this, but long enough that I forgot entirely about the party happening downstairs or about the fact, this was my baby sister's wedding. That this was one of her bridesmaids. I didn't care about any of it. I just wanted to lose myself to this moment, with this woman and she seemed determined to do the same.

We kissed slowly as we fucked, taking our time. I moved my hands over every part of her I could get them on. I wanted to remember how this felt, how she felt, as though I could recreate this if I just had enough of the details committed to memory.

"Fuck." I groaned in her ear as she pushed her hips back against me with more purpose than before. She felt incredible, her pussy tightening around my cock as I thrust into her harder and faster. Her legs were hooked around my back and I was buried deep inside her, as deep as I could go, and it still didn't feel like enough. I could have fucked her all night long and still come up for air wanting more, more of her, more of *this.*

Suddenly, she pressed her head into my shoulder and let out a cry. Her pussy clenched hard around me, over and over again, the pulsing sensations coursing through my entire system. I let myself go too, my body finally tipping over the edge, the release intense beyond anything I'd experienced before in my life. Her body trembled from top to bottom as my cock emptied deep inside her.

We took a moment to extract ourselves from each other. She too seemed reluctant for the moment to end so soon, but eventually, I pulled back, planting a kiss on her lips and brushing my nose against hers.

"That was…" she began.

"Was?" I drawled. "What makes you think in the past-tense?"

She grinned, and wrapping her arms around me tight, pulled me back down on top of her.

"The night is only just beginning, babe," I whispered as my mouth closed over a swollen nipple.

CHAPTER 5

ANNETTE

I gathered my stuff as quietly as I could, tiptoeing around the room so as not to wake the man passed out in my bed. I knew I should have woken him up, said goodbye, at least told him I was leaving, but all I wanted to do was slide into a taxi and head to the airport.

And think about all the incredible things that had happened last night.

No, I never made it back down to the wedding, for which I knew I should feel guilty, but I didn't. I doubted anyone noticed I was gone. Nana would for sure, have done a good job covering for me, letting me get what I needed to out of my system for the night while I came to terms with what she'd told me.

In the bright light of day, away from the lusty evening I had spent with Cole, the reality of her situation was beginning to sink in with an ugly clarity. Ugh…I just slept with Collette's big brother. Oh, the humiliation of it.

Do I tell her?

No. Definitely not. I knew Cole would never tell anyone and neither would I.

I sighed. I wanted to sink back into what that night had given me, a freedom from what I'd been trying to forget, a temporary promise of complete sexual fulfillment. He made me feel beautiful. But last night was gone. And in the cold light filtering in through the crack in the drapes—the future looked bleak, but I had to accept the fact. The most important person in the world to me wasn't going to be around for much longer.

At least she'd given me something solid to cling on to though, something to do for her.

She wanted me to settle down so she could go without worrying about my future. Sure, I could do that for her. I'd been dating casually, keeping an eye out for Mr. Right, but there had been no urgency in my search until now. I glanced over at Cole, laying splayed out on the bed fast asleep, and shook my head. I knew one thing for sure, a man like him was about as far removed from what I was searching for.

But that was okay.

Last night hadn't been about beginning my search. It had been about being with someone through the horror of coming to terms with what I'd been told. He made it a little easier to handle, and we were good...*very damn* good together. I had to admit this. I wondered if all his one night stands were as amazing as last night. The only other time I had a one night stand I *hated* it. A man once told me he didn't care if his one-night stands left without saying goodbye. In fact, he preferred it that way, but I felt used and slutty when he slipped out of the bed and out the door while I pretended to sleep.

Maybe this is why I was doing it to Cole.

I stood over the bed and stared down at him, sleeping so peacefully. My cheeks burned when I thought about how good he was. How much I had allowed him to do to me. That had to be some of the best sex I'd ever had in my life. Part of me wanted to climb back into bed and see where this could go. What we had last night was special. I'd never felt that with any other man.

Then again, he was Cole at the end of the day. Not just my best friend's big brother, but one of the biggest sleeparounds in the city. I couldn't commit myself to someone like him, not when it was one hundred percent certain I would get my heart broken. Anyway, I didn't have time to waste on a guy like him. I didn't have time to waste at all. I had to get my plan going to find someone who would give me what I needed before I lost the most precious person in the whole world.

I pushed this thought to the back of my head. No, I couldn't look at it like that. I had to look at this as a positive thing. Not losing her, but her impetus as the reason to finally get my personal life together and find someone to be with.

I wanted a proper relationship, I really did. Yes, I didn't catch the bouquet, but I wanted the next wedding I attended to be my own. I wanted Nana to be there with me when I got married. I wanted to see her eyes full of pride and joy and know I was the cause of it.

Once I left this room, I intended to put this night with Cole to the back of my mind for good and start my search for a good man. I checked myself in the bathroom mirror, tidied up my hair and the smudges of make-up still on my face, then scrawled a little thank you for a great night note on the hotel stationery and put it on the pillow next to Cole.

Then I headed for the door with my bag hooked over one shoulder.

With my standards high and if the night with Cole was anything to go by, I promised myself I wouldn't settle for anything less than the sexual chemistry I experienced with him. I just had to find the kind of guy who could deliver on everything else I needed, as well.

$\sim$

As soon as I got back to my apartment, after a long flight and a car journey that seemed to go on forever, I texted everyone to let them know I hadn't been kidnapped in the night. Then I called Nana and set up an appointment to see her the next day. After that, I threw myself into my new project.

I started off somewhere obvious, some place my mild hang-over wouldn't get in the way, so I set up a couple of online dating profiles.

I'd never tried online dating before, well, not properly. I had just mindlessly scrolled through some sites and quickly decided it was far too weird to meet someone this way and had gone back to my preferred technique: hoping to bump into someone cute at a party I'd been invited to.

It had worked well enough, but I was at the stage now where most of my friends were married and so were most of the people they hung out with, so finding someone single at one of those events was pretty tough. I had to take some new measures, and this was the best way I could think of to do it.

I curated my pictures, my profile, then put the pieces together, and closed my laptop.

~

I was busy on Sunday. Or rather, I kept myself busy, so I wouldn't have time to think. Laundry, cleaning, grocery shopping. Then I went to see Nana. She didn't want to go into details but it was the big C. The doctors had given her six month. It was a very emotional evening for me and I tried to be strong for Nana, but I just couldn't stop the waterworks.

Nana seemed surprisingly stoic, as she made me a cup of tea and comforted me. She said she had made her peace with God and was ready. The only thing she wanted was to see me taken care of.

By the time I got home, I felt exhausted and went to bed early. When I got back from work on Monday evening I realized there were a couple of messages sitting in my inbox for me.

I bit my lip with anticipation as I opened them up, and what a surprise, I found myself confronted with a picture of some idiot's dick and another message from another fool asking if he could send me his dick pic to check out. I closed the app and rolled my eyes.

This was a less than auspicious start, but two pale, misshapen dicks did not make a failed mission.

CHAPTER 6

I persisted and over the next couple of days, I managed to cultivate a couple of dates who seemed promising. One of them, Leo, worked in law, like me, and seemed smart and funny enough. We chatted for a few days before he invited me out for a drink at a bar across town. I agreed, looking at his kind brown eyes on his profile to remind myself why I was doing this.

The problem was I couldn't drown in them. They were not melted chocolate…like Cole's. Stop it, I scolded myself. I had gotten *everything* I would ever get from Cole. I knew that and so did he. Otherwise, he would have called me. Some tiny part of me had fantasized about him calling me. That part had waited and mourned when he did not.

Time to forget him. He wasn't for me.

As I got ready for my date with Leo, I felt a little flutter in my chest. Maybe this would be it. A guy who worked in the same profession as me, living in the same city? I was surprised we had never come across each other before. Maybe we would talk and realize how close we had come to meeting and laugh at how we never ran into each other, and that would be that. Maybe this would be a story I would tell to our grandkids one day.

There were more things in this world than chocolate pools you could lose yourself in, right?

I sat at a table in the bar, nursing a glass of red wine, texting my nana under the table. Of course, she had insisted on knowing where I was going and whom I would be with. She watched too many true crime shows for her own good, but I appreciated having her presence via text to keep me from getting too nervous about my date with fate.

He was a few minutes late, but I wasn't mad about it. I knew how hectic life could be working in a law office. He had been vague about the one he was actually associated with, but that didn't bother me, either. Maybe he was thinking about moving firms and didn't want to commit to anything?

I got that. The law profession is full of secretive individuals.

He walked through the door and I felt my heart leap as soon as I saw him. Not in excitement. More like nervous, a small panic running through my system, driving me a little crazy. He didn't look too different from his profile picture, which after the horror stories I'd heard was a relief. His hair was a little messier and he had a scrub of stubble, but he had probably been busy at work. I half-leapt out of my seat, waving awkwardly at him.

His eyes focused on me and he headed over. "Hey," he greeted and slipped into the seat beside mine, sliding up just an inch too close to me for a man I'd just met.

NEVER CATCH THE BOUQUET

"Leo?" I said coolly.

"Yeah, sorry I'm late." He yawned, running his hands through his hair and messing it up even further.

I smiled and shook my head. "Don't worry. I get it. Law hours can be tough."

"Right," he replied.

I noticed that his eyes slid away from me as he spoke. It bothered me, but I ignored it. He was likely just nervous, like me. "So, which company do you work in?" I asked, taking a sip of my wine. He was still sitting too close to me and I'd been itching to move without making it too obvious.

"Johnson and Taylor, across town," he replied confidently. "I just came from work, actually."

"Oh, yeah?" I perked up. "I heard they're really competitive over there. You must have worked your ass off to get a job with them."

"It wasn't so hard." He shrugged modestly. "They hired me pretty much on the spot. Guess they really needed someone to take the position, you know?"

"I would have thought lots of applicants would be applying to an august firm like that," I replied, furrowing my brow. "You must have had a great reputation."

"Yeah, well, I've been running my own place for a while," he replied, a boastful edge to his voice.

"Really?" My eyes widened. "That's amazing! What was your specialty? Criminal law?"

He shifted his eyes away from me once more.

Now I felt that little *zing* of worry once again. Something was off about this guy, I could tell.

"Uh, we mostly worked at offices like Johnson and Taylor," he replied. "You know, big places like that. Heralds, for a while."

"But they both deal in completely different fields," I pointed out, confused. "Which type of law exactly do you practice?"

"Uh, I…" He trailed off, clearly not wanting to come out and say it. "I clean," he finally replied.

I stared at him for a second. "I'm sorry?"

"I clean the offices," he replied grimly.

"You clean law offices?" I said slowly. Everything was falling into place now. I tried to re-calibrate myself as best I could. I didn't want to come across as some snob who saw herself as far above anyone who didn't work in law, but he had definitely been trying to lead me to believe he worked in a similar profession to mine. It was the lie or fooling me that bothered me.

"Is that a problem?" he asked with an edge to his voice.

I shook my head. "No, I just thought—"

"Well, you thought wrong," he cut me off, getting to his feet. "I'm going to get a drink." And with that, he stalked off.

I began to realize that this maybe wasn't what I was looking for.

The rest of the night wasn't much better. He got sloppily drunk and wound up trying to put his hand up my dress, then invite me back to my place, at which point I excused myself and got a cab home. I'd had two drinks, just enough to throw into sharp focus how shitty this night had been.

What a creep.

The good thing was I knew what to avoid now. I texted my nana to let her know I was home all right, and felt a twist of guilt deep down in my chest. I had failed her. Another day passed, and I had failed to give her what she'd wanted.

I decided to double my efforts.

I picked up my phone and looked at the app. Leo wasn't the only guy I had been talking to, thankfully. I was also talking to Theo, a firefighter with nice arms, a good smile, and a boyish face who seemed very keen to meet me as soon as possible. And what better way to wipe out the memory of a bad date than to replace it with another one?

I made arrangements to meet up with Theo. He suggested that we go to a coffee shop for our first date, and I agreed at once. I felt glad he didn't need booze to try and supplement our first meeting. Maybe this was a good sign. A guy who took care of himself, so maybe he would take care of me?

That made sense, right?

CHAPTER 7

ANNETTE

I headed down to the café with a buzz of nerves, but also a hint of cynicism at the back of my mind. What if he turned out to be another dead end, just like Leo had been? I'd looked him up online and found a few pictures of him with other firefighters, standing next to firetrucks and posing for newspaper pictures, so I at least knew he wasn't cleaning the firehouse. This would be okay too, but to lie to someone before you even met them? No, a bad start and a very bad sign for a relationship.

He was already there when I arrived, and as soon as I laid eyes on him, I could tell something was off. I couldn't put my finger on it for a moment, but he appeared too eager. Like a puppy that wanted your attention.

"Annette?" He got to his feet at once, greeting me with a hug and a kiss on the cheek.

I was almost choked by the heavy aftershave he wore, something that pulled me straight back to high school dances and insecure boy-men.

"Yeah, that's me," I replied with a smile as I extracted myself from his grip and peered at him closer. He also looked younger than he had in the pictures on his profile. His face was free of lines, his body a little less developed, but maybe he was just blessed with good genes? He was meant to be twenty-seven, so a little younger than me, but maybe a younger man would be what I needed to keep ahold of my own youthful side.

"Do you want anything?" he asked, grinning broadly at me. "Whatever you want."

"Uh, sure, a latte would be nice," I replied, taking a seat.

"Gotcha," he said energetically, and went off towards the counter

I watched him go with a bemused expression. He seemed enthusiastic. Which was nice. I'd been out with plenty of guys who had tried to play desperately cool when they were out with me, and I was glad to have someone who at least didn't feel the need to do that. But...

He joined me once more, and up close, I could see just how young he looked. I furrowed my brow at him. "Sorry to ask," I began, figuring I should get my doubts out of the way now, so we could laugh about it later. "But how old exactly are you?"

"It says on my profile," he replied.

I noticed that he shifted in his seat as he spoke, as though he wasn't quite sure what he had said on it.

"And you're a firefighter?" I asked.

He nodded enthusiastically. "I'm in training. I'm going to be all qualified soon. Just in time for my twentieth—" He stopped abruptly.

I stared at him for a moment as the coffee steamed in front of me. "Your twentieth birthday?" I filled in the blank.

He chewed his bottom lip. "I just really liked your profile," he confessed, blurting out the words before he could stop himself. "I didn't want you to think I was too young for you. I mean—"

"You're nineteen?" I exclaimed.

"I'll be twenty in a few months."

At this point. I burst into helpless laughter. Of course, he was a teenager. The boyish face, the puppy like enthusiasm, the over-applied aftershave. He was just a kid. A *baby.*

"But I'm so much more mature than the girls my age." He grabbed my hand.

I stopped laughing and yanked it away.

"I just think I'd be so much better suited to someone like you—"

"And I think I'd be suited to someone who's not an actual teenager," I shot back. It was funny a few seconds ago, but now I just felt angry. What did he think? I wouldn't find out. Was this what I would have to put up with from now on? One lie after another.

"Aw...come on. You're a bit heavier than I thought you'd be, but I'm not complaining."

Getting to my feet, I tossed some money down on the table. "That's for the coffee."

"You don't have to pay. I invited—"

"If you pay, then it's a date, and I don't go on dates with teenagers," I cut him off, pulling my coat on.

"But—"

"Goodbye and please don't contact me again," I warned, heading for the door. I wasn't much interested in hearing anything else he had to say. He had already pissed me off enough.

As I walked home, I deleted the dating app from my phone. Fool me twice, right? I wouldn't let anyone make me feel like an idiot again. People could misrepresent themselves online any way they wanted, but I had no intention of indulging their fantasies of who they wanted to be for a moment longer.

For some reason I couldn't stop my mind from incessantly drifting back to the night I'd spent with Cole in Vegas. It seemed so far away now, so distant. As if it had happened to someone else. Or had been just a fantastic dream.

And why wouldn't I feel that way? Cole hadn't bothered to so much as reach out to me since then. Sometimes, I couldn't help wondering with some regret if I should have hung around a little longer, woken him up, and seen where it led. But I hadn't and the chance was lost. And that was that.

I tried to figure out why I couldn't feel anywhere near the chemistry I had with Cole with any of the guys I'd met since. Not one could measure up. Not even a bit. I was simply going through the motions with all of them.

Maybe there was a specific alchemy to that night. Maybe because I'd been not only been in a great deal of pain and upset, but also a bit tipsy, I'd been just vulnerable enough to open myself up to him and an experience like that. Or maybe it was because what I did was unnatural. I didn't want to go out with these men, but was only doing it because of Nana. The truth was I didn't want to find a man. I wanted to curl up on the floor and cry at the thought of my nana leaving me.

I arrived back at the apartment, and mentally ticked "online dating" off my list of methods to find a man. I had to try something different. I forced myself to go online and look at some speed-dating meetings for singles in my area. At least then, I wouldn't be wasting days talking to people pretending to be something they weren't.

Before I had a chance to talk myself out of it, I signed myself up for a couple of events and crashed straight into bed. It was only early evening, but I felt as though I needed all the sleep in the world to give myself the energy to get out there once more. Who knew dating would be so exhausting? No wonder I'd never done it before.

The speed dating night came around a couple of days later, and I found myself wishing that I could have talked to Collette about all of this. She was my go-to for help and support when it came to dating, but she was still away on her honeymoon, and I didn't want to disturb her. Besides, I would have to tell her the truth about why I was doing this, and I hadn't spoken to anyone but Cole about it until now. The thought of sharing it with someone else made me want to throw up. It would just make it all the more real, and that was the last thing I wanted.

Even Gia who was my second go-to was away for a whole month on an Australian outback expedition with her husband. Only rarely did she find Internet cafes and she just about managed to do a Facebook post then, telling everybody about all the exciting things she was seeing and doing. So I did feel a bit abandoned and out of sorts as I came out of the shower.

I picked up a new dress for the evening, dark blue, with capped sleeves and a hem that flared out around my knees. It was cute, but also a bit conservative. I had no idea the kind of men I would be meeting tonight, and I didn't want to give the wrong impression.

I was in it for a long-term relationship.

I arrived at the venue, a slick, modern building, with signs that led through to a meeting room where the event would be taking place. I took a deep breath and headed inside.

Tables and chairs set up on either side facing one another had been arranged to snake around the room. I looked around the room, and felt my heart sink as I realized there wasn't one guy in here I would have given a second look if I had been out on the town. I also saw a lot of people looking a hell of a lot like I did, tinged with desperation, hopeful that this would be the end to their search. I noticed a couple of men looking me up and down, but I swiftly averted my eyes towards the coordinator at the door who was pressing a nametag and a pen into my hand.

"Here you go." She smiled at me. "Put this on, so people know who you are."

I did as I was told, slapping the cheap adhesive over my special new dress with a heavy heart. Before I had a chance to think about slipping out and going home to order myself a calorie laden takeout, the coordinator clapped her hands together and stepped into the middle of the room. I noticed a wedding ring glinting on her finger. I wondered if it was real, or if she had to wear it to make it seem as though these kinds of events actually worked.

"Okay, ladies and gentlemen, welcome," she called out.

The room quietened down. Apparently, a few of the people here had already started their speed-dating, chatting each other up before the event had even begun.

"Please take your place at one of the tables around the room," she continued, and there was a rush of sound as people sat down. I made sure to slip into the seat closest to the door. It was an easy escape if I decided I didn't want to stay after all.

"Ladies, you'll be staying where you are, and gentlemen, you'll be making your way around. You'll have five minutes with each date. When you hear the bell, you move to the next table in a clockwise motion." She grinned widely. "No matter how much you like the girl. Remember to mark your card. If both of you mark that you would like to meet again we'll put you in touch. It's as simple as that. All that is left to is to wish you good luck and ask you to enjoy your evening." She stepped back and took her place at a desk at the front of the room as though she was an exam adjudicator making sure none of us cheated. The bell rang.

A man took a seat opposite me. He looked almost bald and the few strands he had, he'd combed sideways across his shining head. His eyes drifted down my body, making my cute new dress feel like a bit less special. I felt the urge to get up and leave again, but I fought it. I had to give it a go since I was already here.

"So, hi," I greeted, putting on what I hoped was a welcoming smile to make him feel comfortable. Perhaps the major creep vibes I got from him were just accidental run-offs of his nervousness. I had to hope that, at least.

"Hey." He didn't take his eyes off my cleavage.

I began to wish I had brought a jacket so I could wrap it around my shoulders, but as it was, I just had to sit here and hope he would figure out something better to do than just gazing longingly at my tits.

"You've attended an event like this before?" I asked.

He leaned forward, as though he was about to tell me a secret. "Yeah, and let me tell you," he eyed me with a hunger that made my stomach turn. "The women in places like this are just as fast as the dating."

"What the fuck do you mean?" I snapped, leaning back and away from him.

"Hey, I didn't mean to insult you." He held his hands up. "Just that if you're coming to a place like this, you must be pretty desperate for…"

He left the final word unsaid, but he didn't need to come out with it. I already had a firm grasp on what he thought I was so desperate for. And frankly, I had no interest in sitting here a moment longer, listening to some asshole tell me what I did or didn't want.

I got to my feet and headed for the door.

The coordinator came to try and intercept me, but I guess

she must have seen the look on my face because she held her hands up and let me sweep past her.

And just like that, I was out in the corridor once more, all alone again. The entire evening had been a write-off. I should never have come out here in the first place. What had I been thinking? Of course, the guys who were there would just be looking for a quick, easy lay. None of them were exactly coming out to a place like this to fill themselves with long-term love.

I wondered how lucky the lot of them got, if any of them in there had actually come with the hopes of finding someone to really connect with. Some part of me wanted to duck back in there and announce the intentions of that man to every woman in the room, but I assumed my sudden exit would be enough to get every woman in that place looking at him sideways.

The walls felt as if they were closing in on me. I needed some fresh air, and I darted for the door. Outside, I tipped my head back and inhaled a great lungful of air, filling myself up on it. It was right then when I heard a voice I recognized.

CHAPTER 8

"Annette?"

I opened my eyes, praying it wasn't the one person I didn't want to see right now, but there he stood.

Cole in front of me, gazing at me with a look of mild amusement and surprise on his face.

Last time I saw him, I was sneaking out of the hotel room in Vegas while he'd been fast asleep. Though, judging by the look on his face, he didn't harbor any hard feelings towards me.

"What are you doing here?" he asked.

I glanced back inside the building, debating if I should lie about my true reason for being here, but I figured I might as well be up-front with him. I had nothing to lose. "I was in there for a speed-dating night," I confessed, with a grimace.

He raised his eyebrows at me and chuckled. "Should I assume it didn't go so well?"

49

"No, it didn't." I shook my head with a heavy sigh. "It was pretty shitty, to be honest with you. I thought it might be a good way to meet some new guys, but the first one I spoke to made me get up and leave."

"What was the problem with him?" he wondered curiously.

I rolled my eyes. "He pretty much just came out and told me that he was only there because he thought that the women who went to events like that would be easy."

Cole spluttered with laughter.

"Glad you find it funny," I said sarcastically.

"I'm sorry." He raised his hands in apology. "That's just...a hell of a hook-up strategy, that's all."

I sighed. "Trust me, if you'd had to deal with the dating stuff that I have in the last couple of weeks, you wouldn't be laughing either."

"Come on, you can't just leave it at that. What's been so hard?"

"I tried out dating apps," I admitted. "And the first guy I met told me that he worked at a law office but then turned out to be a cleaner there."

Cole's eyes filled with mischief and laughter. "Seriously?"

"Seriously." I nodded. It seemed odd, but I actually felt glad to have someone to share my dating woes with. I knew it was silly, but it felt like such a relief to get all this off my chest, to know someone else could see it for the ridiculous nonsense I had always known it was. "And then the second guy I went out with turned out to be a nineteen-year-old kid."

Cole's eyes rounded. "Ouch. That sucks."

"Tell me about it." I groaned. "And he called me a bit on the heavy side."

His eyes moved over my body and darkened suddenly, reminding me of that night. "The young can never be expected to appreciate the finer things in life."

"Well…" I looked away from him awkwardly. Something had shifted between us again. I was stone-cold sober, but my attraction to him still felt as potent as ever.

"You want a lift home?" he asked. "I was just dropping something off at the offices over there, but I have nothing else to do for tonight."

I eyed him. It would save me the cost of a cab home, along with the horror of sitting in my apartment looking back over the bad dream that this night had turned out to be. "You sure?"

"Never been surer of anything in my life," he drawled, his eyes hooded.

I felt a little flicker of excitement at the thought of him taking me home. Which was ridiculous, because the two of us were nothing more than a one-night-stand with the unfortunate complication of my friendship with his sister. "Yeah, that would be great, thanks," I mumbled.

He grinned and gestured to his car, a gorgeous, midnight-blue Corvette. "Come on, you'll have to give me directions." Opening the door, he waited for me to slide into the front passenger seat.

That flicker of sexual heat and excitement came back again, as I caught a whiff of his wonderful aftershave.

He climbed in next to me and pulled away smoothly.

For a moment, a strange silence hung between us, as though we were both trying to avoid mentioning the fact that we had spent a night together not so long ago. A night that had been one of the best things to happen to me in recent memory, if I were being honest with myself.

"Uh, just take a left up here," I directed him, knowing very well the route I had sent him down would take longer than the most direct one. I just didn't want to be alone quite yet, especially not when he was the one keeping me company.

"How's your grandmother doing?" he asked suddenly.

I felt touched that not only he had remembered she was ill, he sounded like he cared. "Uh, not too great." I shook my head. I called her this morning from work to tell her about my speed dating venture. She had sounded worryingly woozy and maybe even a little out of it, but she'd insisted it was nothing to worry about. She blamed all the drugs she was on. "But she's keeping up with her treatment," I finished up. I didn't want to have to talk about this. I wanted to move on. "What about you?" I asked. "How are you doing?"

"Still recovering from the wedding, I think," he replied, giving me a sideways look.

"Yeah, me too," I agreed. My hands curled into fists on my lap. "Right up here and then straight on." I snuck a look at him. I wondered if I should mention the fact I had sneaked out of the hotel room before he had woken up, and had wondered ever since whether I should have stayed. Was he mad at me for leaving him? Did he think it was funny? He had hooked up with a lot of women, but maybe he wasn't used to being the one who got left behind.

"Right here is fine," I told him quietly as we drove up to my apartment building.

He drew to a halt and glanced at me.

"Thanks for the lift," I said, lingering in the car longer than I needed to. I wasn't sure what I was doing, but I didn't want to go up to my apartment and be alone, to face up to the reality that I had just fucked up another potential chance to meet someone I wanted to be with.

Also, to face up to what I did the last time I didn't want to be alone. I had ended up in bed with him. Which had been a bad idea. Hadn't it? "Is your sister still on her honeymoon?" I blurted out before I could stop myself. I wasn't sure why there seemed to be this distinction in my head, but if she was still away, I could convince myself that whatever I did now existed in some sort of magical limbo between the consequences and the actions.

"I think so."

"You want to come up for a drink?" I asked, as I half-expected him to shoot me down.

Then the slowest smile I'd ever seen appeared and curled upwards onto his face. "Yeah, a *drink* sounds good."

"Just to say thanks for the lift," I said hurriedly.

His eyes twinkled. "Okay."

I felt a flush run up my neck; he'd seen right through me, but you know what? I didn't give a damn. As he climbed out of the car, I knew exactly where this night would go, and I didn't mind one tiny little bit.

CHAPTER 9

COLE

I followed her into her apartment building, all the while marveling at the good grace that had not only dumped me in front of the one woman I hadn't been able to get out of my head the last two weeks, but while she was in need of some company.

"So, how's your dating life been?" She glanced over her shoulder at me as she unlocked the door to her apartment.

I knew that she was expecting me to reel off a list of names I'd been hooking up with, but the truth was I hadn't been that interested in fucking around at all. Waking up to find her gone from the hotel room had been more of a shake-up than I'd expected and I'd been thinking about her a hell of a lot ever since. I shrugged. "Not nearly as exciting as yours, by the sound of it."

"Trust me, I'd settle for something boring." She glanced over her shoulder as I stepped inside.

I laughed. "No, you wouldn't."

She turned around to face me and furrowed her brow. "What do you mean?"

"I mean, you hooked up with your best friend's brother at her wedding in Vegas," I reminded her. "I somehow doubt that boring would work out for you."

She went bright red and looked away from me.

I thought for an instant I might have overstepped some line, but then I noticed a small satisfied smile curl one end of her lips, and I knew she thought of that night with the same emotion I did.

"What would you like to drink?" She went into her cupboard. "I have red or white wine. And maybe an old bottle of scotch I won at some raffle three years ago."

"White sounds perfect," I replied, as I took in her apartment; small, but well-appointed, decked out in shades of ochre and bronze and beige. Stylish, chic. Like her.

She poured us both a glass, then directed me towards the couch in the living room.

The place smelled like her, clean and fresh, a hint of jasmine lingering in the air. I liked it. Reminded me of having my nose buried in her neck, how good she'd smelled, how good she had tasted. "So, beyond the dating, what have you been up to since the wedding?" I asked.

"Honestly, nothing very exciting," she admitted with a shrug. "I thought that dating was meant to be interesting, but I'm starting to believe it's just a long con put together by people who write rom-coms."

"Perhaps you're going about it the wrong way." I raised my glass to her.

Her eyes widened. She had on a pretty dress, her make-up done for a date, and it seemed like the universe had wrapped her up prettily and then just dropped her on to my lap. It couldn't have been more perfect.

She rolled her eyes "Oh, silly me. Thinking we might have something in common. Of course, you've never had any trouble landing a decent date."

I grinned at her. "You want some tips?"

She took a sip of her wine and eyed me over the top of the glass. "And what might those consist of?"

I pretended to rub my chin and think. "Well, I would start by quitting speed-dating. Stick to people you already know."

"Like who?" she asked with such a sexy, knowing smile, I knew that the two of us were floating along on the same wavelength. The two of us had been dropped into each other's' lives tonight by pure chance, and now I was here, at her apartment, drinking wine like the two of us had been back at the hotel in Vegas. The universe had thrust us back together, and who were we to deny the whims of the universe?

I cocked my head at her. "Like someone you already know you'll have a good time with."

She licked her lips. "Like who?"

"I'm more of a show, not tell, guy," I purred, shifting towards her by an inch.

She put her glass of wine down.

I caught her hand and brought it to my mouth, brushing my lips over her fingers ever-so-lightly. She gasped and bit her lip, and I knew her mind was in exactly the same place as mine. And that was all that mattered.

I leaned towards her, placing the glass of wine down next to me, the booze already forgotten with the promise of her once again. I slipped my hand around the back of her neck and drew her towards me, pressing my lips against hers, tasting the wine on her lips as they parted and allowed my tongue to slip into her hot mouth.

Pulling her onto my lap, I wrapped my arms tight around her delicious curves. A familiarity mixed in with the newness as I made out with her on the couch. Something about Annette made me think I was in serious trouble. Maybe the forbidden element about hooking up with my sister's friend, although to be fair that had been something that had never turned me on. I just saw it as a troublesome complication. Or maybe it was because she snuck out on me. Something about the tables being turned on me seemed to have flicked a switch inside my head, a switch I had been unable to flick back to off ever since.

She looped her arms around my neck cradling my head as I sucked on her tongue. I skimmed my fingers down her back, over her thighs, underneath the hem of her dress. I knew she'd dressed up for someone else tonight, and if I were honest, the idea of her with another man infuriated me, but knowing I was the one getting the full benefit of her failed date-night look made my cock swell in my pants. I pushed my thigh between her legs.

"Bedroom," she gasped in my ear, her wine-scented breath warm on my skin.

I stood up, scooping her into my arms as I did so. She giggled and clung onto me for dear life, pointing me in the direction I needed to take her. The first time we hooked up, she had been so sad, so broken, her cheeks tear-stained, but now she sparkled with life. Her playfulness came off of her in delightful waves. I kicked the door shut behind us, just in case she had a roommate. Planting a kiss on her lips, I threw her on to the bed.

She yelped and bounced.

What a beauty. I climbed on the bed.

CHAPTER 10

COLE

"Come here." She pulled me down on top of her, kissing me again with all the passion inside her, pulling at my shirt until she had eased it up and over my head.

I tossed it aside and she ran her hands greedily over my back, my chest, my shoulders. Thank God, for the hours I'd spent in the gym, because judging by the appreciative noises she made as she touched me, she liked what I had on show right now. "Now, you," I told her, as I flipped her around so she was on top of me and pulled up the hem of her dress.

She eagerly tugged it over her head and tossed it aside. So there she was, a goddamn goddess, sitting astride me in nothing but a bra and a matching pair of lacy panties.

I couldn't stop the low animal growl rumbling deep in my throat at the sight of all that beauty.

She ground her covered pussy on my thigh, and I could feel how soaked the crotch of her panties were. It drove me crazy. I let my hands roam down to her waist, her skin felt tantalizingly soft beneath my fingers. I moved my fingers to the inner seam of her panties, tracing the line that ran over the crease of her hips, watching as she tipped her head back and moaned at the feeling of my fingers against her skin. Almost viciously, I tore her little lacy panties away. Her soft pussy was naked against my skin. Just the way I liked her.

"Now spread your legs and show me your pretty pussy."

She opened her thighs shamelessly and showed me her sweet, sweet pussy. It was so wet and pink my mouth began to water. There was an urgency inside me like I'd never known to taste her honey again. I wanted it so badly. I'd never felt that with any other woman. "Jesus, Annette. I need to taste you again," I muttered.

Obediently, she rose, moved up, and lowered her pussy onto my mouth. I sucked her whole sex into my mouth, and ate her pussy until she screamed uncontrollably. I held her tightly while she went over the edge. The way she came apart above me was so beautiful it hurt. I gently sucked her clit until she stopped convulsing and the last of her orgasm had rolled over her.

She looked down at me, her lids heavy, her eyes glazed. "Wow, Cole. That was amazing."

I licked the thick cream running down her thighs and she looked at me with wonder in her eyes. "You really like eating me, don't you?"

"I'd be a fool not to, Annette Parker. You taste like the ripest, sweetest summer peach."

"Now it's your turn. I'm going to suck you off, but first I want to feel you inside me," she said with a smile, as she slipped backwards until she was straddling my thighs. Unlike our first time when she was feeling vulnerable and upset, this time she seemed happy to take some control for herself.

I wasn't complaining. Too many women I've been with just lay there, hoping that looking cute was enough to fulfil the deal. I didn't have the heart to tell them it was just boring.

Annette undid my jeans and pushed them down my legs. My cock was already so hard it was peeping over the waistband of my underwear. She took the hard flesh into her hand, and with her eyes fixed on it, she stroked it eagerly. Her fingers looked so good wrapped around my erection. She flicked her tongue out over her bottom lip, as she dry humped my leg as if she could hardly wait to have me inside her.

I knew how she felt.

"Will you get inside me now?" she asked, her voice sweet, but impossibly sexy.

I nodded. "Hang on. I've got a condom in my jeans pocket."

"No need," she said, and grabbed one from the dresser. Tearing it open, she rolled it down over my length. As she did, I swiftly reached up, undid her bra, and tossed it aside, so I could see her tits bounce while she rode me. As soon as she had the rubber on, I pulled her forward and sucked a nipple into my mouth. I was feeling especially horny so I sucked it hard, but by her moans, I knew it was just the right kind of rough. I let her nipple go with a pop and moved to the other one. Her cries became louder.

She hadn't finished the job of taking off my jeans, and they were bunched around my ankles. I kicked them off as she pushed me back down onto the bed. Shifting forward and looking deep into my eyes, she took hold of my thick cock.

Positioning it over her entrance, she slowly impaled herself down on top of it. Her body looked incredible, but the way my cock disappeared had an unexpected effect on me. It made me feel possessive of her pleasure. I wanted to own her body. To be the only cock that travelled into that sweet, wet hole.

"My God! I forgot how fucking big you were," she groaned as she planted her hands on my chest and pushed herself all the way down.

She felt amazing, her pussy was soft, slick and oh so tight, but I couldn't take my eyes off her face, the euphoria written all over it was enough to burn the moment into my memory forever. The sight of her so blatantly using me for her pleasure was incredibly hot.

She rocked herself back and forth on top of me. I reached up and held her hips tight as she moved, guiding her slowly. She was looking deep into my eyes, staring at me. It reminded me of Vegas. That had been intense too, but for completely different reasons. This... this was full-on lust, need, desire, nothing else at play.

We both knew exactly what we were doing this time. No bullshit excuses of too much alcohol, being in Vegas, or trying to run away from something painful. This time, we were just two bodies in need.

I let her ride me for a while, allowing her to set the pace, while I took in the holy sight of her on top of me. Her eyes were closed and her head tipped back, her full breasts moving in time with her pace.

She didn't seem in any rush, as though she could have taken all night to get there and been happy with how she'd spent it.

I, on the other hand was already nearly bursting. After a while, I slid my hand between her legs and began to play with her clit, stroking her softly in time with her bouncing on me. She let out a moan, and it seemed to push something in me, something that had been teetering close to the edge, finally tipping out over the top of it.

I wrapped my arm around her and sat up, thrusting into her hard; she sank her fingers into my shoulder and kissed me deeply, her teeth catching on my lip as we made out. She was moaning softly with every plunge into her, her body taking all of me. I pulled away from her and looked her in the eyes, watching them glaze with pleasure as I slammed again and again into her. I went to kiss her again, but she wouldn't let me, shifting an inch too far away from me, her gaze burning brightly in to mine as though this was what she wanted.

To see me. To watch me tip over the edge into the abyss.

"God," I groaned, and I felt my cock twitch inside of her, my balls tingling as my orgasm roared through me. I kept my eyes on hers, and watched as she gave in to the same pleasure, her pussy clenched around my cock, her body giving in, crumpling into mine helplessly as her climax overtook her. She let out a stream of cries, as though all the pent-up energy was escaping her all at once. She kept grinding herself hard against me as I spurted inside her.

For a long while neither of us moved. The only sound in the room was our ragged breaths and our hearts pounding. Eventually, we unwrapped ourselves from one another.

She slowly lifted herself off of me and slid down on to the bed beside me. "Holy shit," she gasped, staring up at the ceiling, sprawled stark naked on the sheets.

"Bathroom?" I asked.

She pointed to the door opposite the bedroom. "Right there," she replied.

I headed off to dispose of the condom before I returned to join her on the bed. Her eyes had drifted shut by the time I arrived back. Lazily, she reached out to run her fingers over my chest and to my surprise, even though I'd only just finished fucking her, my pulse picked up as soon as she touched me.

"If you want to make a break for it now, I get it," she said, the words sounded as if they had been carefully rehearsed.

I recognized it for what it was. Attack was the best form of defense. She was worried I was only staying out of politeness. "That's more your scene, not mine," I reminded her.

She laughed. "Yeah, okay, I get it. I shouldn't have snuck out without waking you. But it was Vegas. We're not in Vegas."

"Oh, so that is your excuse?"

She opened her eyes and looked at me. "It's not an excuse," she protested. "That's a perfectly valid reason. People hook up all the time in Vegas and never see each other again." She smiled suddenly, sweetly, innocently. "Besides, I had a world of shitty dates to get started on."

I grinned. "And how's that been working out for you?"

"Well, I'm in bed with the last guy I hooked up with, so I guess I'm going backwards instead of forwards," she admitted. She pulled the covers over herself, resting her head comfortably back on the pillow behind her. Her hair was a beautiful mess over the pillow.

She exuded something light and carefree, something I had a hard time finding in a lot of the other women I'd been with. "I'm glad to hear Vegas worked for you," I remarked casually.

She glanced over at me. "What do you mean?"

"Well, you found someone there." I gestured to myself with a faux-cockiness.

"Yeah, but I think Collette would skin us both alive if she found out what was going on here," she pointed out. "You got any single friends to speak of? Ones who are less related to my best friend?"

"I have a few," I replied. I could think of a couple off the top of my head, but I felt sick to my stomach at the thought of those assholes getting close to her.

"You have to set me up." She sighed. "I could use some help."

"You're over this just like that?" I shot back, surprised by how much her statement hurt.

She furrowed her brows at me. "Was there something to get over?"

"I should damn well hope so." I grinned, playing it cool. "You telling me you've had better than what we've just had?"

"You're so arrogant." She shook her head and laughed, but she didn't argue with my assessment. "So are you going to set me up with one of your eligible friends or not?"

I frowned. I was starting to get annoyed at the thought of her with other men.

"Why are you frowning? We are not right for each other and not just because of Collette either. You are...loose and fancy

66

free…I want to settle down and get married as soon as possible. I was hoping tonight would get you out of my system."

"And has it?"

She bit her lip. "Honestly?"

"Of course."

"No."

It felt like the big black clouds parted and the sun came shining through. I had to stop myself from grinning from ear to ear like a fool. I cleared my throat. "We should go back to Vegas."

She eyed me for a moment, clearly trying to figure out if I was kidding or not. "You serious?"

"Yep." I nodded.

"Why?"

"We had a lot of fun there, didn't we?" I reminded her.

"Yeah, but—"

"So…it's obvious. The only way to get something out of your system is to over indulge until that thing that was special and rare becomes commonplace and ordinary."

She grinned at me. "What are you saying?"

"I'd like to fly you out to Vegas for a couple of days before I give you access to my long list of single friends."

Her eyes widened.

"It's the right thing to do. It just wouldn't be fair to my

friends if you're still carrying a torch for my...fucking big dick."

She hit my arm. "You're no gentleman."

"Hey, I was just repeating what you said."

She giggled. "You really mean it?"

I nodded. "Dead serious. All on me. This is the only way we would be sure that you're really ready to settle down with a lesser cock...

She hit me again.

"And," I continued, "I wouldn't be shortchanging my poor friends." I propped myself up and looked at her. "You in?"

She glanced at me, clearly weighing up just how obviously bad an idea this was in her head, but I didn't see why I shouldn't throw it out there. She was incredible in bed, and I knew I would never forgive myself if she settled down with someone else before we'd had a decent amount of fun together. Anyway, that was what I told myself. I wasn't ready to admit to myself that she was different from all the others. Very different. And I was actually quite crazy about her.

"You do realize it's a totally ridiculous idea, don't you?"

"I don't hear you saying no," I pointed out. "Come on, luxury hotel, all expenses paid, orgasms around the clock, a big cock..."

"All right!" she agreed, laughing. "All right, you've twisted my arm."

I grinned. I felt as though I'd just landed the deal of a lifetime. "Trust me, you won't regret it," I promised her.

She laughed. "No, I don't think I will," she agreed as she rolled on to her side and stretched her arm out over my chest. "Now, are you ready to have that fucking big cock of yours sucked off?"

I grinned. Was I ever!

CHAPTER 11

ANNETTE

I still didn't know what I had been thinking, agreeing to go to Vegas with him for a wild weekend. I didn't do things like that! Period.

Maybe it was just the disaster of the last few dates, matched with the incredible sex we'd just had when he'd asked me. Maybe the promise of getting away from everything that had been going on in my head recently. Besides, he did have a point: if I intended to settle down, I might as well get everything out of my system while I still had the chance. Especially since, he had offered to help set me up with one of his numerous bachelor friends afterwards. Although, when I thought about it, the idea didn't seem appealing at all.

Maybe because it was all to do with him, he had something I couldn't quite put my finger on, but it was as potent and powerful as they came. He was the first man who made my knees weak when he kissed me.

Friday came and I got out of work early to meet him at the airport.

"You ready to fly?" he asked.

He greeted me with such a wide smile, I swear my heart flipped double-time in my chest as soon as I laid eyes on him. He looked even better than normal, freshly shaved and dressed in a laid-back tee and jeans. I couldn't believe that this man had really offered to sweep me across the country for a dirty weekend. I still didn't quite understand why he was doing it, but I guess it didn't matter. All that mattered was we were doing this and I was more than looking forward to spending time with the man who'd made me come harder than anyone else ever had in my life before.

"Yeah, I am," I agreed.

Cole grabbed my bag and we walked up to check-in together. He had purchased us first-class tickets.

I raised my eyebrows as we were swept into the fancy waiting lounge. "Remind me what you do for a living, again?" I remarked as a smiling attendant came up with a glass of wine for us both.

"Heading for partner at my law firm," he replied.

I grinned. "No wonder Collette got into it as well," I commented. "She saw the kind of life you can live doing this stuff."

"Or maybe we were just both raised with the same sense of noble justice," he teased.

"Ah, you haven't heard what the rest of the world thinks of lawyers, have you?" I countered, taking a sip of the booze. It was expensive and I felt incredibly up-market just being here with him.

"You're going to tell me, huh?"

"Lawyers are liars."

He rubbed his chin thoughtfully. "Don't you work in a law firm too?"

"Ours is a small firm that does a lot of pro-bono work."

"Of course. Our firm works on the basis that everyone is innocent until proven guilty...even me," he said softly, his eyes sparkling.

"Point taken. I apologize for jumping to conclusions," I conceded.

"Apology accepted," he drawled suavely.

I changed the subject. "How can you take time away from work if you're in-line for partner?"

"Because I'm a workaholic and I've put in enough hours there to last ten lifetimes."

I smiled. "Right. Have you told Collette what we're doing?" I asked

He shook his head and raised his glass to me. "I don't normally keep my sister informed about my love life and I don't intend to start now. This is just between us."

"Just between us," I echoed, touching my glass to his. I bit my lip when I saw the way his tongue flicked out over his bottom lip to lick up the last drop of the wine from his mouth. Hell, the last time I saw him do that... I couldn't wait to kiss him.

The flight was surprisingly quick and comfortable, but I supposed I could expect this when it came to flying first-class. His lifestyle was what I could have earned for myself if I had had the nerve to go for his level of hard work, but at heart I was a social justice warrior and to be perfectly honest, I had never quite had the right amount of drive to go for the jugular.

Still, I had to respect his ambition. It was admirable.

We arrived about nine, and I knew I should have been exhausted by the flight, but I felt more energized than anything. I knew this was crazy and that was why I hadn't even told anyone what I would be doing or where I would be going. If anyone found out they would immediately remind me about this man's lady-killer reputation and I didn't want to have to sully this trip with remembering that.

I was here for a good time, not a long time, and I knew he felt the same way.

A car waited for us when we came out of the airport.

Cole pulled the door open for me and let me slip inside.

"Wow! I was wrong. You are a gentleman, after all." I smiled at him as he joined me.

"Don't get ahead of yourself," he warned, reaching over and letting his hand rest on the inside of my thigh.

My heart picked up even faster in my chest. I couldn't believe this incredible man really seemed to want me as much as he did. Maybe it had something to do with the fact I had made it clear I planned on settling down soon, and now he was focusing all his energy on making sure he got what he wanted from me before I slipped through his fingers. Though maybe, I wasn't giving him quite enough credit. After all, we had already hooked up twice, and yet he'd deigned me worthy enough to earn this ridiculous trip at his expense.

I gasped when I laid eyes on the hotel.

The place that Collette had been married in, that had been impressive enough, but this was on a whole other level. It towered above us as we stepped out of the cab, glowing in the evening light, lit up with neon. When we stepped into the foyer, I was taken aback by the sheer, over-the-top luxury of the place. Gold details everywhere, a fountain sitting next to reception, a perfectly-coiffed receptionist smiling up at us as we approached her.

"Hi, my usual?" Cole said.

She nodded, her eyes briefly sliding across to meet mine as she typed his name into the computer. "Here you go," she slid an envelope with the card keys across the counter towards us.

Cole thanked her, grabbed them and took my hand.

"We'll take your bags up in a moment," she called after us as we headed for the elevator.

"You have a usual room here?" I cocked an eyebrow at him.

He shrugged. "Nice to know I can trust somewhere for a good night's sleep." He grinned down at me as the doors slid shut. "Or a lack of it."

CHAPTER 12

ANNETTE

He opened the door and we were not in a room, but in such a fancy ass suite, my jaw nearly dropped when I saw the place we would be staying over this weekend. It was stunning, with the biggest bed I'd ever seen in my life, draped in expensive sheets. A few subtle but handsome paintings adorned the walls, and a bottle of champagne was waiting for us on a balcony beyond.

"This is insane." I shook my head and glanced to him. "You really paid for all of this?"

"Since this is supposed to be your last blowout before you settle down for good, I thought it should be fun, at the very least."

"This is way more than fun. This is downright decadent," I said drifting towards the balcony, making note of the fact that the bed was so large you could spend the whole weekend in it while being secretly glad about it.

"Champagne?" he suggested, following me out.

I turned around and nodded happily.

He popped the cork and poured us both a glass.

I took a sip, the chilled bubbles exploding on my tongue, and sending shivers everywhere.

"To a wonderful weekend." He touched his glass to mine.

The way his eyes flashed at me even in the dark was enough to make my skin prickle with excitement. The last time I'd been here, it had been all about the pure celebration of love. I had a feeling tonight would be anything but pure.

I turned to look out over the city below me, and he slipped his arm around my waist, I leaned back against his hard length with a sigh of contentment. He had such an easy way about him, as though he had done this a thousand times before. But what was truly amazing was what we shared felt so utterly us. As if this was how it was always meant to be. I caught myself in my crazy thought. This was nothing but a dirty weekend, I reminded myself sternly.

"So you come here a lot?" I said aloud.

"Sometimes," he replied. "It's for sure where I go when I want to blow off some steam. Everyone knows me back home, and it's nice to get away from that for a while, you know?"

"Get away from your reputation," I snorted. "I wouldn't have thought that would be possible."

"Remember, innocent until found guilty," he murmured.

Suddenly, I was aware of his thumb tracing the spot where my pulse fluttered in my throat.

"You would be surprised how far away I am from the skirt chasing demon you seem to think I am."

"Would I?" I glanced up at him, my heart racing in my chest.

He placed his glass down on the edge of the balcony. The wind tousled his hair and dropped it on his forehead, making him appear unbelievably sexy. He reached a hand up and carelessly pushed it away. He just had no idea how breath-takingly gorgeous he was

"Yes," he replied firmly. "I'm not a kid anymore. I don't expand that kind on energy on dating anymore."

"No," I whispered.

"No," he said with a shake of his head.

"Then what is this weekend all about?"

"This weekend is all about you, Annette Parker, and only you," he said as he whirled me around and pressed his mouth against mine.

He tasted of the expensive champagne, smooth and intoxi-cating, as he pulled me close to him at once. I melted into his arms, loving the feel of him against me, the comforting warmth of his body so close to my own. I put my glass down and wound my arms around him, and suddenly, standing here above the city, with this man who had made sure this weekend would be perfect for me, I felt so grateful. I wanted to show him just how much this meant to me.

He deepened the kiss, but before he could take things any further, I pulled back. He gazed down at me, his brow furrowed. "What?"

"Shhh," I said and sank to my knees in front of him.

"Here?" he asked, that notorious grin appearing on his face.

"Mmmm," I replied.

"I want you naked," he said, his eyes glittering with a challenge he thought I wouldn't have the guts to meet.

I rose to my feet, unzipped my dress, and let it pool around my shoes. The cool air hit my body, but I didn't feel cold. I felt excited by the possessive lust in his eyes. I took off my bra and his jaw actually clenched. Then I hooked my fingers into the waistband of my panties and pushed them down. I stepped out and stood in front of him wearing nothing but my blue high-heels. I raised my hands, flicked my hair away from my neck and his eyes followed the movement hungrily.

I could see I was driving him crazy and it made me feel powerful.

Taking a step towards him, I pressed my naked body against him. "Is that better?" I whispered in his ear.

"Turn around and show me your ass," he ordered.

I turned around and walked up to the railing. Spreading my legs, I held the railing and bent down, giving him an eyeful of my pussy.

"Jesus, Annette," he muttered.

I smiled in the dark before I went back to him and crouching down began to undo his pants. Pulling down his underwear, I wrapped my fist around his cock. He was rock hard and absolutely massive. It aroused me to know just watching my naked body was getting him off. I pumped him a couple of times, very close to my mouth, warming the throbbing flesh with my breath. I knew that if anyone stepped out onto their balconies above us, they would be able to see exactly what we were doing, but I didn't give a damn.

I just wanted to show him how thankful I felt for what he'd done for me.

He tipped his head back as I leaned forward and took him into my mouth. I could taste the salty drop of pre-cum on the tip of his cock, and I swirled my tongue around him hungrily, tasting every part of him. Above me, he groaned and slipped his hand through my hair, letting it rest on the back of my head, encouraging me, but not forcing me to take more of him than I wanted to. I slid my mouth a little further over his cock, inch by inch, covering what I couldn't with my mouth with my fingers.

"Play with yourself. I want to watch." His voice sounded so hoarse I could barely understand him.

Obediently, I let my other hand slide down to my pussy. A part of me couldn't believe I was doing this. I had never allowed myself to do anything this naughty in my life before, but with him, it felt as though it was second nature. I found my clit. I was already swollen and soaking wet so I stroked myself gently as I moved my mouth further down his cock to take as much of him as I could at once.

"Fuck, Annette," he rumbled, his voice so low and guttural it sounded like it was coming from somewhere hidden deep inside him. It was so shockingly different from his usual tone that my eyes swiveled up to his face. His mouth was open, his breathing ragged, and his eyes roamed over my pale body wildly. Knowing I had turned him into this desperate beast sent another surge of arousal through me as I rubbed my clit harder.

I took my hand tentatively away from his cock and slid it around his ass, sinking my fingers into his flesh and guiding him deeper into my mouth. Until him, I had never really enjoyed giving a man a blowjob. Yeah, sure I did it, but I never enjoyed it. I didn't like the taste, I didn't like the loss of power, as if I was being used, but with Cole, it was the opposite. Not only did I enjoy his taste, but it made me feel powerful. It made me feel as if I was the one in control.

I moaned softly around his cock, sealing my lips as he flexed himself deep into my mouth. I started to suck softly, running my tongue up his underside, as his fingers pressed a little harder into my head. He was really, *really* enjoying this, I could tell. Which was exactly what I wanted.

He began to slowly thrust his cock in and out of my mouth, fucking my face, letting me get used to the feeling of his erection slipping deep into my mouth. I gagged the first time, so he immediately slowed down and allowed me to set the pace. Soon enough, I was surprised to find I could take him deeper and deeper into my throat, further than any man had ever made it before. He was letting me command this situation, and I adored that about him. I loved that he wasn't here to make a point, to fuck my face and be done with it. He wanted this to be enjoyable for me, and I totally *loved* it.

I moved my fingers around my own clit with more purpose, feeling myself inch closer and closer to the edge. It seemed incredible but going down on him was getting me off, feeling his cock filling my mouth the way it would fill my pussy soon enough. I wanted him to come. I wanted to feel him tip over the edge inside my mouth. I loved the feeling of him being helpless because of how good I was at this. I had never wanted it more in my life. I sucked harder, and then slipped my mouth up, lapping at his tip and flicking my gaze up to meet his. He was gazing down at me with lust in his eyes, dark and needy. I slipped my mouth off him so I could speak, just for a moment:

"I want you to come in my mouth," I breathed. "Some in throat, some on my tongue."

He let out another one of those deep growls of pure arousal. I knew he was telling me he was close, and I felt another surge of desire rush through my body. Rubbing my clit harder, I felt my own orgasm getting close as I sealed my lips around his cock and began to fuck him relentlessly. I reached my hand between his legs and stroked his balls. Then, as though he could hold it back no longer, he came with a roar. His hot seed spurting deep in my throat into my stomach

"Holy shit," he gasped as he finished in my mouth. I swallowed down every last drop until I felt my own orgasm crest and break within me. It wasn't as intense as it was when he was giving them to me, but it was enough to satisfy me for now. A start. A good start and a promise that this weekend would be unforgettable.

Moments after he withdrew from my mouth, a knock came at the door. We both glanced around, and I felt a rush of panic that someone had seen what we were up to and had now come by to complain.

He pulled his pants up, before doing the same to me. "Don't look so devastated. It's just our luggage."

I let out a sigh of relief which turned into a yelp of surprise when he grabbed me and threw me over his shoulder. He gave my ass a smack as he carried me back into the suite and deposited me unceremoniously on the bed.

I lay on the bed with my legs splayed open.

"I want to see you exactly like that when I come back," he instructed before he closed the door and went to see to the luggage.

I grinned to myself. I felt as though the person I usually was had been left behind in the city, and now this version of me had come sweeping in to take her place, someone powerful, in-control, smart and sexy— ready to do whatever it took to please her man. Not that he was *my* man, of course. No, nothing like that. But for the next few days, he was all mine. And I had every intention of making the most of it.

Cole came back to find me in exactly the same position he had left me. The first thing he did was eat me. Then we spent the rest of the evening in bed, talking, drinking champagne, eating room service food, and fucking relentlessly. Of course, we slept late the next day and by the time, I woke up, he was returning from the gym, freshly showered and wandering around the room half-naked, as he got dressed.

He glanced over at me. "Morning." He grinned, throwing himself down on the bed next to me and planting a kiss on my shoulder.

"Good morning to you too," I said awkwardly. He looked so lovely and fresh while I just smelled of sex.

"God, you smell amazing," he said. "It makes me want to fuck you all over again."

"No, I don't and don't you dare. Seven times in one night is quite enough. I'm still so sore I don't know if I can walk straight."

He leaned on the bed. "All right. How about some breakfast?

I know a place near here that does the best breakfast in the city."

"Sounds perfect," I agreed, rolling out of bed and going towards the shower. The last time we shared a morning in a hotel room, I had sneaked out afterwards, but now I wanted nothing more than to spend the rest of the day with him.

CHAPTER 13

ANNETTE

Cole took my hand as we walked out into the city together. This was only the second time I had ever visited Vegas. The first had been such a whirlwind for Collette's wedding that I'd hardly had time to take it in. It was wonderful to revisit it with Cole. He was caring, charming and humorous and...oh, he just made everything sparkle.

We stopped in at a diner not far from the hotel. Unlike everywhere else we'd been so far, this place was kitschy, cute and cheap. I was glad for the chance to be able to pay for something for a change. "You put your money away," I ordered firmly, as he reached for his wallet. "Least I can do is pay for something."

"Nah, don't worry about it. This weekend is my treat."

"Please, I want to," I said softly, as we slid into our booth that looked out over the bustling street beyond, the view to hundreds of people going about their day. Normally, that would have made me feel slightly uncomfortable, as though

I should have been keeping up with them, but in this moment, with this man, I was perfectly happy to wish them good luck and curl up closer to the most fantastic adventure of my life.

"This place doesn't seem like somewhere you would like," I commented, waving my hand around as the waitress brought us coffee.

He cocked his head at me. "No? Why not?"

"Just seems like you have a taste for the finer things in life, not the diner ones."

He chuckled. "All right, that has to be the worst pun I've ever heard in my life. Besides, I know I'm a few years older than you are but I was a student once, too. I still have a soft spot for cheap, crappy food with a good view."

"Yeah, this is a nice view." I looked out on to the street again.

"Actually, I was referring to my breakfast date." Looking deep into my eyes, he slipped his hand to my knee beneath the table.

I felt myself flush. He was so damn *smooth*. None of the guys I'd dated before had been anything like him, and I had to admit it was kind of working for me.

When we finished breakfast, we headed over to a casino on the other side of the city, one that he promised me was the most fun we would have in all of Vegas. I had never really been one for gambling before, but I was surprised to find what a good time it was, goofing around the slot machines and the gambling tables with him.

"Hah!" I exclaimed as I won another small jackpot on the slot machine. "I'm going to buy that hotel we're staying in at this rate."

He raised his eyebrows. "That's what you'd use the money for?"

"Why not? Then I might let you stay in my hotel for free," I teased, as I collected my tokens.

"Stay for free? I'd rather pay and have you join me," he replied with a twinkle in his eyes.

"I thought this was our last hurrah together."

"My motto is never say never," he said before taking my hand and nodding towards the blackjack board. "Come on, I want you to be my lucky charm." He tugged me in the direction of the tables.

I followed on behind him. Who was I to deny him what I wanted? I realized I had a big-ass goofy grin on my face as I went after him, surprised at what a good time I was having. My nana would love it here. My heart hurt when I thought of her, but I knew she'd want me to be out having a good time over anything else, especially since I would soon have to settle down with someone who wouldn't be able to hold a candle to Cole. This thought made me feel strangely glum, but I plastered a smile on my face and pretended nothing was wrong.

Cole won ten thousand then lost fifteen and I dragged him away. "Come on. Let's go. I'm not your lucky charm," I said feeling a little sad that I hadn't been the lucky charm he wanted me to be.

He pulled me towards him. "Are you kidding? Right now, I'm the luckiest guy on earth."

My heart nearly stopped and I stared up at him in shock. Did he just? No, of course, he didn't. He was just being charming. "You just lost fifteen thousand dollars, Cole," I said lamely.

He shrugged. "Did you have fun here?"

I nodded. "Well, at least until you started losing all that money."

"Then it was worth it." He grinned suddenly. "Anyway, if you really feel bad about me losing all that money, I know how you can make me feel better."

"How?" I asked suspiciously.

"I'm a show kind of guy," he said.

We went back to the hotel and he showed me exactly *how*.

We headed out for dinner that evening to one of those Asian fusion places not far from the hotel.

"Cheap diner in the morning, then a place like this in the evening," I remarked playfully as we were led to our table.

"I'm a man of many tastes." Cole waved his hand in a faux-mystical fashion.

We took our seats opposite one another and I cocked my head at him. "So, I have to ask," I began.

He looked up at me expectantly. "Yeah?"

"Why did you do all this for me?" Part of me didn't want to hear the answer to that question, given that it might undercut the beautiful time we were having so far, but another passive aggressive side of me simply had to know.

"Have I been hauled in front of the Annette Parker one woman judge and jury again?" he mocked.

"It was just a question," I shot back, but I felt more than a little on the defensive.

He reached over to take my hand. "Would you please relax? I'm doing this because I have a good time with you," he explained gently. "There's no ulterior motive to it. You're going off the market soon and I'm taking full advantage."

I bit my lip. I knew I shouldn't have asked. "And that's what this is, then?"

"Of course, it is."

"I have to say, if more of my single life had been like this, maybe I might not be in such a rush to find someone." I had meant to make it sound like a joke, but it just came out sad and bitter.

"Hey, no reason you can't be in a relationship and do stuff like this," he pointed out.

"Not that you'd know much about relationships." Jesus, why did I keep digging myself deeper and deeper into this hole.

"You'd be surprised." He shrugged, as the waiter approached with our menu.

I took the menu and smiled my thanks. "Would I?"

"I don't know why you have this odd impression of me. I've dated people before. A couple of my relationships have even lasted close to six months." He sounded a little defensive, as though he was trying to prove something to me.

"Really?" I furrowed my brow at him. "Collette makes it sound like you spend all your time screwing around."

"Yeah, well, Collette doesn't know everything about me," he replied. "I have a life that she doesn't know about. The reason my relationships don't work out is not because I hunger for new flesh all the time, but because I always valued my career over any relationship and at some point that generally drove all my girlfriends crazy."

"And what will you do when you're partner?" I asked. "When you haven't got as much to work for?"

"Oh, then I'll launch my own company just so I don't get too comfortable."

"You're crazy, you know that?" I shot back.

"Some people would just call it ambition," he pointed out.

"Never had a lot of that myself," I admitted. "I mean, I like my job, but I'm happy where I am right now."

"You're a paralegal, right? Same as Collette?"

"Yeah, same as Collette," I nodded. "And I'm happy sticking around there. I look at people like you, and the thought of all that responsibility terrifies me."

"It's not as bad as all that."

"Yeah, that's easy for you to say," I pointed out. "You've been doing it for years now. You've never had the lazy gene to worry about."

"The one thing you are not is lazy. I've had lazy girlfriends so

89

I should know." He shrugged. "Maybe your career isn't your priority."

"True, but I'm not sure what is."

"You still have plenty of time to figure it out."

"I'm not so sure about that," I replied, thinking of my nana. I wished, suddenly, that I could have convinced her I would be well on my own when she was gone. For so long, I had relied on her to take care of me, to look after me, to provide what I needed in life. I was thirty and I still hadn't done enough to assure her that I would be totally fine if she wasn't in my life.

The waiter came to take our order and I decided it was best to drop the maudlin topic. The weekend was meant to be fun and besides, I didn't want to get too attached to him. The best part of all of this was not having to play the dating game, being able to be honest about who I was and what I wanted. As opposed to ducking from every bit of honesty, he'd asked for. It would be good practice for what I was looking for when it came to dating for real. Be honest and live it like you meant it instead of this play-acting that most people were doing.

Dinner was delicious, and we made our way back to the hotel slowly, taking in the ambience of the nightlife as we went. He took my hand. It thrilled me to know everyone around us would look at us together and see us as just any other couple.

I yawned as soon as we were back in the hotel room. I hadn't had a chance to try out the luxurious bath yet. I had every intention of trying out each and every of those tiny bottles of free toiletries. They smelled divine. "I think I'm going to take a bath."

"Mind if I join you?" he asked.

I looked at him from under my lashes. "Don't see why not," I murmured as I swiftly pulled off the sexy black dress he'd been ogling at all night long. I carelessly tossed it on the floor and watched with satisfaction as his eyes trailed up and down my bare-ass naked body.

"You weren't wearing any underwear?" he asked incredulously.

"You coming?" I asked playfully as I turned away. I could see him in the reflection in the floor to ceiling glass walls.

CHAPTER 14

For a few seconds, he stood there staring at me, the he started pulling off his shirt and kicking off his jeans.

As I swayed my hips seductively I changed my mind about the bath. The shower room was huge and more appropriate for what I had in mind. It was almost as though it had been made for a couple of people to fuck in. This entire hotel seemed to have been built to make room for people to screw around, the luxurious beds, the enormous balconies, the champagne, the bathroom. Like Vegas itself, this hotel was made for sin.

I switched on the rain shower then stepped beneath the pouring water, leaving the door open, and he soon joined me. I turned my head to look at him. His erection was already jutting out aggressively. I grinned.

Cole wrapped his arms around me from behind, grinding himself into me, running his hands over my breasts, my belly, and my thighs. "I love your body. It's like a red rag to a bull. I see it and I go mad."

I tipped my head back, making room for him to kiss my neck.

He brushed his mouth over my skin and up to my ear, nibbling softly on the lobe. "Mmm," he moaned against me. "You taste so good…"

"I still think I need you to clean me up," I murmured, handing him a little bottle of shampoo.

He quickly squirted out a little into his palm, and began to massage it into my scalp. The deftness of his fingers as they stimulated my skin drew a moan of sheer delight from my mouth. Then he slipped his other hand between my legs and found my clit. He stroked it gently as the water cascaded over my body, his fingers in my hair and against my pussy, the sensations almost more than I could wrap my head around.

"Fuck, that feels sooooooo good." I groaned, grinding myself restlessly against his hand. In fact, my entire body was reacting to him, meeting him, needing him.

The warmth of the water and the heat of his body were setting all my nerve endings on fire. I couldn't get over how amazing it felt. For his part, he seemed enormously fascinated by every part of my body, as though each and every inch of me needed exploration and attention.

He switched on the hand-held shower head. Then he moved his fingers lower, and inserted them deep into my pussy. Easing me back an inch or two, he held the shower head so that the jet of water cascaded directly over my clit. The mesh of sensations were so intense I could feel them pushing me close to the edge.

"There you go, baby. Get good and ready for my cock."

I closed my eyes and moaned.

He wrapped his fingers into my hair and tugged my head back so my eyes opened and I stared up at him. "I want you to come with me inside your sweet cunt," he growled.

My knees practically quivered out from underneath me. "Yes," I agreed feverishly.

"Hold the shower head," he instructed, before he grabbed a condom from where he had placed it on the shower stand. He didn't even take his fingers out of my slit as he sheathed himself, getting me good and ready for his cock.

The jet of water continued to massage my clit as he grabbed my hips and pulled them back so my bottom jutted out. Then I felt his tip pressing up against my pussy. With one forceful thrust, he was inside me. I let out a cry of pleasure and surprise, the sound echoing around the enclosed space. How could it be that he still felt this good to me? Normally, once I'd been with a guy a few times, the thrill of having him enter me would wear off.

But with Cole, it was as intense as it had been the very first time.

"I love the way your little pussy clenches all around me," he murmured in my ear.

I pressed myself back against him, as hard as I could, the water drumming up against my clit, lighting up every inch of my sex. The cascade of water from the rain shower and jets of water beating my clit together with the movement of his hands and made me feel as though he was taking care of every inch of my body all at once, touching me, feeling me, caressing me. I couldn't get enough of it. I wasn't sure I would ever be able to.

He moved deeper into me, grinding his hips with more purpose as he thrust in with long, deep strokes into my pussy. His fingers were moving with more purpose now.

I was all but helpless to his touch, lost to the pure pleasure of having him handle me like this.

How could it feel this damn *good?*

Long gone were the guilty thoughts about this being my best friend's brother or the doubts over him having the reputation he did. All that mattered was how good we felt together.

I was getting close to my climax and my body ready to give over to the rush of pleasure. He snaked an arm around my waist and pulled me in close to him. Flattening his hand against my belly, he pulled me down towards him, pushing his cock so deep into my pussy I gasped with the sensation. The sound was washed away by the water crashing all around us. He ran his mouth up along my neck, across my shoulder and suddenly bit into the soft flesh there.

That was all I needed to finally get myself there.

I opened and closed my mouth, the water flowing over my face, as I came, trying to give shape and sound to the impossible sensations pulsing through my body. My pussy clenched hard around his cock, again and again, and I felt myself collapse into him. Moments later, his cock surged violently inside me, and he found his own release while buried deep in my pussy.

He slowly withdrew out of me, kissing my shoulder where

the flesh still throbbed. Then he got down on his knees, pulled my pussy lips apart kissing and licking me.

To my surprise, I came again. The contractions were so powerful he had to hold me, or I would have fallen. He held me for a few moments as I got my bearings back as he stroked my skin.

"See you in the room," he whispered. Then, with apparent reluctance, he slid out of the shower. I heard the sound of the bin opening and knew he was disposing the condom. I let the water cascade over me, eyes closed, pretending that it was his hands, caressing me, touching me, learning every inch of me.

Once my legs had stopped trembling, I wrapped myself in the fluffy robe hanging by the door and went into the room. I grinned when I laid eyes on him. He was splayed on the bed, naked and utterly confident in his body. He had good reason to be. He was like a God. I had never been with a man who was so taut and lean.

"Well, hello there," he greeted me.

"Hey," I said, suddenly strangely shy.

"You want to get room service? I don't feel like going anywhere, but I want some good wine."

"Sounds perfect," I agreed, sliding down on the bed next to him. This felt so comfortable—maybe a little too comfortable.

"You look so cute just out of the shower," he remarked.

"Yeah, with no make-up and soaked hair," I joked uncomfortably. "I'm irresistible."

"I don't know why you keep saying that like it isn't true," he replied with a slight frown.

I raised an eyebrow at him. "You always know what to say, don't you?"

He raised himself on his elbows. "Two can play this game, you know. I could accuse you of fishing. You can't possibly not know how beautiful, you are."

I licked my lips. No one had ever called me beautiful. Attractive and kind of pretty, but never beautiful. Was he being sincere? A little voice in my head kept whispering that he must say this kind of thing to every woman he swept away for a romantic getaway, but when I looked into his eyes, I could see he was getting annoyed with my constant distrust of his motives. I licked my lips and ignored the voice in my head. I shouldn't let it get in the way of having a good time. Not when things were going so well. "I'm sorry. Let's start again, shall we?"

The cloud passed instantly from his face and he smiled. "Well, hello there. You look so cute with your hair all wet."

I touched my hair. "Thank you," I whispered.

He bolted up, caught my hand, and tugged.

I fell on top of him.

I lay on top of him as he ordered us some wine. When it arrived, we sat out on the balcony together. It was amazing sitting in the dark sipping expensive wine with the man I could only have dreamed about. "This is amazing," I sighed. "The wine, I mean."

"Hey, what about my company?" he asked, grinning at me.

I nodded gravely. "That's not too bad, either."

"I can't believe I never spent any time with you before this," he remarked, taking a sip from his glass.

"I think Collette's been making a solid effort to keep you away from all her female friends," I pointed out.

He seemed surprised. "She did?"

I nodded. "I know that if she knew about this, she would chew both of us out for it. She thinks you're just going to hurt the women you end up with."

"You've got your facts wrong. To start with, I've never zeroed in on any of Collette's friends, and more importantly, I'm not in the business of hurting women. They always have a great time."

"I can attest to the second fact," I said raising my glass to him.

"Maybe you can defend me to Collette," he suggested. "Maybe encourage her to set me up with one of her friends. I kind of like the brunette with the blonde streaks in her hair."

Unconsciously, my hand reached out to my hair, but I managed a nervous laugh. This joke was a little too close to home. "Yeah, I don't think that's going to happen. I'm not telling anyone about this."

"No?"

"No." I shook my head vigorously. "Too complicated and awkward. As my best friend's big brother, you're meant to be off limits to me."

"Collette's married now," he pointed out. "You don't think she'd be a little more open to us dating?"

"Besides, you're working for a completely different...umm... type of law firm to mine," I reminded him. "I doubt either of our bosses would be too delighted if they found out that we were together."

"Wait till I'm partner." He grinned at me. "Then I'll just pluck you away from your pure and self-righteous firm and hire you to work at our predatory place."

"Hmm, and I get the feeling that your intentions would be less than pure," I remarked.

Cole chuckled. "Yeah, you might have found me out there. So what you're saying is I have no hope at all?"

I glanced over at him, smiling, playing this little game with him. "None."

"None?"

"None," I repeated.

"That's a crying shame," he said, as his arm encircled my waist once more, his fingers slipping into my bathrobe, to find the bare skin inside. "I suppose we should make the most of this weekend, shouldn't we?"

"Yes, I suppose we should," I agreed, just as our lips met again, as I lost myself to his passionate kiss once more.

CHAPTER 15

COLE

"I can't believe it's over already." Annette sighed and pressed her head to the window as the plane came in to land.

"Yeah, back to the real world, huh?" I remarked lightly, but I felt a little twist in my stomach. I knew exactly how she felt. I didn't want this to be done yet. Not by a long shot. I wanted to turn the plane around and fly back to Vegas, back to the weekend we'd spent together, and relive every moment.

"You going to stick to your end of the deal?" Annette glanced over at me.

I cocked my head at her. "What deal?"

"The one where you set me up with some of your actual eligible friends," she reminded me.

My gut burned. "Of course, I am," I replied. "Man of my word, aren't I?"

"Awesome." She flashed me a smile.

Quietly, I wondered how on earth she could let go so quickly of the time we had together. Didn't she want more too? I thought it had been special. Hell, I had tried my hardest to make it feel that way, but she was already figuring out how she would move on, looking to a future with one of my fucking friends. I turned away from her and pretended to look at one of the air hostesses.

Soon, we were back at the airport once more. I helped her to get her bags onto a trolley. This was it, but I couldn't let it be the end. She smiled at me awkwardly. I knew she was trying to come up with something polite to say.

"I had an unforgettable time with you," she blurted out suddenly.

I felt my stomach clench. For the first time she wasn't hiding behind a mask of indifference or trying to play it cool. She was being truthful. We *had* spent an incredible couple of days together: fucking, talking, gambling, eating, and laughing. I had a feeling it would be hard for me to shake how much fun I'd had with her.

"Yeah, me too." I took a deep breath. This was my opportunity and I was grabbing it with both hands. "Look, Annette," I began, "I know what we agreed on, but maybe we could—"

"Hey, Cole!"

I recognized that voice. Brent from my office. I turned around, furious at the interruption. He was grinning at me while striding eagerly in my direction. He was the senior partner's son. This was the guy who'd never had to work for anything. Everything handed to him on a platter. He was also slow on the uptake, but everybody put up with it because of who he was.

"Hey, Brent," I greeted, my voice sounding tight. "Listen, we're in the middle of something."

Annette shot me a strange look, almost as if she was hurt or angry, though I couldn't imagine why.

"Oh, right," Brent said, and instead of getting the clear message, he glanced between us eagerly. "I'm off to France. Where are you guys headed to?"

"Oh, we're not going anywhere," Annette replied for me.

I noticed she was smiling a little too wide at Brent for my liking.

Brent glanced at me, but his attention was really focused on the woman in front of him. "So you're Cole's girlfriend, eh?"

"Oh, no, no," Annette denied instantly, shaking her head so hard, her hair slapped her cheeks. "Uh, I'm best friends with his sister."

For some reason this explanation pissed me off to no end.

Brent looked at me. "Oh, yeah?"

"Yeah, we just ran into each other." I shrugged. I hated being forced to play it down and pretend I hadn't just spent the weekend with this woman.

"In that case..." Brent extended his hand to Annette. "I'm Brent."

"Annette," she replied, taking his hand.

He hung on to her hand for just a moment too long.

I wanted to reach over and tear their hands apart, but I knew it would have infuriated Annette.

NEVER CATCH THE BOUQUET

"Since I don't have to worry about competition from Cole here, it is okay if I ask you out?" he asked in his usual, *the whole world is my oyster and all I have to do is reach and take it* attitude.

"Well, I'm an in-demand woman," Annette joked, shooting me a look. "Who knows who might sweep me off my feet?"

"Maybe me?" Brent suggested, flashing her a cheesy smile to match his cheesy line.

I could feel my fists clenching even as I fought the urge to reduce his teeth count.

She cocked her head at him in that sexy way she had. "You live in the city?"

Brent nodded. "I know you guys are in a hurry, so I won't keep you, but before I go, can I have your number?"

For a second, Annette did not do anything, then she scrambled around in her purse, and handed a card over to him.

"I'll call you," he promised, grinning like a Cheshire cat at her, before turning to nod at me. "See you at the office, Cole."

I felt too shocked to respond. I could not believe they had exchanged phone numbers right in front of me! I watched in disbelief as he happily headed off across the airport.

Annette nudged me. "Hey, look, you're already helping me get a date! I've never given someone my number like that before. I always thought it would be cheesy."

Didn't seem to mind the cheese when it came from him. Thank God, it was only the voice in my head.

"Yeah, guess I am," I replied, my voice sounded more like a snarl. "Umm…Keeping up my end of the deal, right?"

"You sure are." She nodded.

"Yeah, sure looks like you got yourself a date." Just saying the words made me even angrier.

She looked at me sideways. "Is everything all right?"

I forced a smile. "Yeah, sure. Everything is just fine."

"Anyway, I should be getting back to my place…"

"You want to get a cab back together?" I suggested.

She shook her head. "Nah, we live on the opposite sides of town. I don't want to hold you up any longer."

"Okay," I replied, handing her bags to her.

We walked to the entrance of the airport in a strained silence. I wondered what she was thinking.

At the doors, she lingered for a moment. "Thanks…For this weekend. I really appreciated it. It was extremely kind of you."

"No problem." I nodded. "Seems like you're going to be spoken for soon enough."

"Fingers crossed," she gushed, but there was an odd edge to her voice, as if she was putting on an act even she didn't truly believe in. "Right, bye then."

And with that, before I could say anything else, Annette turned around and walked quickly out of the airport.

I lost count of the people who passed me by with their

luggage and careless chatter because I stood there for such a long time. I wanted to make sure she got well ahead of me. To give her time to get away from me because what I really wanted to do was run after her, bundle her into a taxi, and take her back to my place.

I wanted her to give me a chance, instead of that fool, Brent.

CHAPTER 16

ANNETTE

I cried in the taxi. It wasn't sadness. It was fury. I felt so angry with Cole my hands were shaking. He was ashamed of me. After all the bullshit he'd said about how beautiful I was, he didn't even want to introduce me to Brent! The taxi driver was nice, he handed me a box of tissues and told me his daughter was always crying about the men in her life too.

His kind words washed over, but in the end, I calmed myself down by recognizing that I had only myself to blame. I had brought this on myself. I knew when he invited me that I was tempting fate, getting way too close to the source of the flame for my own good, but I found myself not caring.

Everything we had done hadn't been the elements of any dirty weekend, it had been the beginning of a relationship, and now I was fighting the urge to call him up and tell him to get his ass down here so we could actually enjoy the rest of the night together. I could confess my feelings for him, stuff the stupid thing with Brent, and just admit that I only wanted him.

Yet, he'd made what he wanted clear by not even wanting to introduce me to someone from his office. He just wanted sex from me. What a fool I'd been while falling for all his carefully rehearsed patter about how beautiful and perfect I was. *Ugh.*

He was probably already planning the next trip with a new girl. In the same room, in the hotel where the staff knew him. Suddenly, I remembered the blonde air hostess on our flight back and my heart twisted with jealousy at the thought of him looking at her. The way she had smiled at him and the way he'd smiled back at him. God…

As soon as I was back through the door, I knew who I had to talk to.

Collette would know what to do. She was the only person with an inside track to the both of us, and she would be able to tell me what I was meant to do.

She'd been due back from her honeymoon yesterday. She sent me a text to say she would be calling me today, but I couldn't wait for her call. I flopped down on the couch and took a deep breath. I dreaded this conversation, but I knew it was only right to get my priorities and my loyalties right again. I needed to tell Collette the truth. I just hoped I wasn't about to break her newly-wedded bliss by telling her I'd been with her brother.

She was going to chew me out, and I deserved it. I had broken a cardinal rule by hooking up with her brother. How much should I tell her? My mind raced over the last couple of days. Phew, we really did some X-rated stuff together. I swiftly censored the most explicit stuff in my mind. I didn't want to talk about that to anyone, and she certainly wouldn't want to hear it.

I dialed her number and lying back on the couch, looked up at the ceiling. My eyes were unfocused, my mind racing in a hundred different directions at once. Normally, I would have called Nana to talk to her about this stuff, but I knew she would have been disappointed to hear I'd been wasting time with a man who would never marry me. I couldn't handle hurting her like that.

"Hello?" Collette's voice caught me off-guard.

"Uh? Uh, yeah, hi," I greeted.

"Annette? Are you all right?" she asked, sounding concerned.

"Yeah, I'm fine," I assured her at once. I infused enthusiasm into my voice. "Hey, so how was your honeymoon? Was it amazing?"

"It was great, thanks," she replied. "We can talk about that in a minute. I can tell something's up. You're going to tell me what it is or am I going to have to tear it out of you?"

"Yeah, I have something to tell you," I admitted, pinching the bridge of my nose between my fingers and wincing.

"Hit me," she said crisply.

I heard the creak of her couch as she settled in and relaxed for some gossip. "I have—okay, I don't know how to say this, uh…" I mumbled.

"For God's sake, just tell me, won't you?" she encouraged impatiently.

"All right. Uh...I have feelings for your brother," I blurted out, wincing even as the words came out of my mouth.

She fell silent for a long moment, and I could hear the cogs turning in her head as she tried to make sense of what I had just told her. "Are you kidding?" she asked quietly.

"No."

"Has something happened between the two of you?" she demanded.

"Uh, yeah," I decided to leave it at that.

"Jesus Christ," she muttered.

"I'm sorry." I tried to make it better. "I didn't mean for it to happen, I really didn't—I wasn't thinking. At least that first time."

"Hey, hey, I'm not mad at you," she said gently.

"You're not?" I asked, relief pouring into my body.

"No. Not at all. I'm just...worried for you, that's all."

I sighed.

"Oh, hon, Cole's just not the kind of guy you want to catch feelings for," she sadly told me. "And look, I'm saying that as his sister. You should really put some space between you two and get him out of your system."

"I don't know if I can, anymore," I admitted miserably. "I don't know if I even want to."

"Oh, my God. You can't be serious, babe! Cole is great for a one night stand, but forget anything long term. You need to find someone who's going to give you what you actually want," she continued. "I hate to hurt you, but my brother isn't ever going to give you that."

"I know you're right, Collette," I wailed. "I should never have let this happen." Now that I was away from him, everything I'd been trying so hard to ignore was creeping back into my head. He slept around, he didn't settle down, he never wanted anything like that. But somehow, fool that I was, I had managed to convince myself that things were different with me. He could be that man for me. The last few days had been so incredible, so special. It would just take a little time to come down from it.

"Yeah, you shouldn't have," she agreed. "But it has happened now. Just remember the old trick. Replace the man and reduce the pain. Do you have someone else to distract you?"

"Uh, no…" I paused. "Uh, I guess I met this guy, Brent? I gave him my number..."

"There you go. Put all your attention on him," she urged. "My brother has a reputation, honey, and I know that he's earned it. And quite frankly, I'm pissed that he would drag you into whatever game he's playing. I'm going to call him today and give him a piece of my mind, Honestly, it's not like there aren't enough girls for him to play around with, without him fishing from my small pool of friends."

I winced. "Oh, please Collette. Don't say anything to him. It will only make it worse. Besides, it was not his fault. He was just trying to be nice."

"Be nice?" she spat. "You have a really twisted idea about what being nice is all about."

"Please Collette. I just want to forget it ever happened and how can I do that if you rake it all up again?"

"Okay, I won't say anything. I'll be hard, but I'll do it for you. Now, you go out there and get that guy, Brent."

"I guess you're right," I agreed. But when I thought of Brent, I didn't feel that delicious rush of excitement and adrenaline I did when I thought about Cole.

"Trust me, I am," she promised confidently. "Now tell me about this new guy. Come on, get your mind off my brother. He's a loser anyway."

I sighed heavily, and tried to dredge up what I could remember about Brent to convince her that I really could move on from Cole. But the truth of the matter was that I wanted nothing more than to be in Cole's arms again, to give myself over to him and let him have me the way I hadn't been able to get enough of this weekend.

CHAPTER 17

COLE

I drummed my fingers on the arm of the couch, while I waited for her to pick up the phone. This was a dumb idea and I was almost sweating, but I simply couldn't let her go.

I had imagined the weekend in Vegas would probably be enough to get her off of my mind. Familiarity had always bred contempt for me, but all that had done was make things worse. I wasn't sure what it was about this woman that had landed her so utterly and completely lodged inside my brain.

I had hooked up with plenty of girls before, enough to earn myself quite the reputation, and none of them had gotten into my psyche like Annette had. It was one of those songs stuck in a loop, playing incessantly in my brain, relentless and impossible to shake. I kept seeing her in shower, in the bed, in the restaurant, then in the airport, holding prick's hand.

We had parted as friends, but fuck being friends with her. I want her to be my woman.

This was about more than just sex. A good fuck, I could get anywhere. But there was something about the way she looked, the way she talked, the way she didn't take my shit that had me hooked to her, well and truly. And I was more than a little mad at myself for falling so hard for a girl I knew was not that interested in me. Hell, the way she hung on to the scumbag's hand. It made my blood boil all over again.

Having said this, it was a good thing it was Brent's number she got. He wasn't exactly likely to sweep her off her feet. He was a pretty dull guy, but then I remembered how he always had good-looking women on his arm at company do's, so maybe he offered them something I couldn't. I could only hope that whatever it was, Annette wasn't searching for it.

The phone stopped ringing and Annette's voice came through. "Cole?"

"Hey, Annette." I felt a wash of calm pass over me as I heard her voice again. I hadn't realized how much I had actually missed her voice until this moment, but now I could see. It felt as though some part of me had clicked into place again, some small section of my mind filled in. Not that I had fallen for her, or anything. Not that I ever did that.

"Hey, what's up?" she asked, her voice changing, she was clearly in a hurry to be somewhere else.

"I was just wondering if you wanted to get together at some point." I fiddled with the glass sitting next to me on the couch. I was home from work early. I had been doing a decent job distracting myself from her by throwing myself head-first into work for the last week, but when I was home in the apartment alone, I couldn't stop thinking about her.

"Oh?" She sounded surprised.

Now, I realized how much this just sounded like I was asking her out. "To talk about the kind of guys you want me to set you up with," I added quickly.

"Oh." She cleared her throat. "Well..."

"How about tonight?" I suggested, without thinking about how desperate I might sound.

She fell silent for a moment. "I would love to, but I actually have a date with Brent this evening."

I frowned. Fuck, he moved fast. That was precisely the opposite of what I wanted to hear. "Where are you guys headed?" I asked, hoping it was somewhere cheesy, somewhere I could convince myself Brent would have no chance of actually wooing her.

"Oh, La Maison Douce."

My heart dropped. Yes, the classic dating place for guys in our line of work. Expensive, impressive, and the waiters treated you like a king. Getting laid after a night out there was almost guaranteed. "What a coincidence," I found myself saying. "I have a date tonight and we're going there, too."

"I thought you said you wanted to meet with me tonight?" she said, sounding confused.

Shit. Caught out in my own lie. "Yeah, I thought we could just meet for a drink or something first," I amended my statement.

"Oh, right," she said quietly.

"Maybe we could meet you guys there?" I suggested. "Make it into a double date."

"Uh, sure, I guess so," she agreed, though she sounded far from certain. "Brent is picking me up at about seven. I guess we'll see you there then?"

"Yeah, you will," I replied with certainty. I knew that it was childish, but I wanted to make sure her date with Brent wouldn't go well. Not necessarily to sabotage it, but if I could just remind her of what a good time the two of us had had together, maybe that would be enough.

"See you later," she said before hanging up.

I sat back in my seat, wondering what the hell I'd just gotten myself into. I basically invited myself along on her date with her new man. A man who worked with me, no less. What the fuck was I thinking? This was crazy… beyond ridiculous.

Of course, I could have called her back and told her that I'd made a mistake, that my date was tomorrow night. Apologized for the mix-up and told her to have fun, but I didn't. I couldn't. I couldn't even sit still. I stood up and began to pace the floor. Fuck, what a mess I'd gotten myself into. This was my karma for all the times women wanted me and I didn't want them.

After a while of wearing out my carpets, I sat back down and picked up my phone again to look over the contacts within for someone I could hit up for a date at the last minute.

CHAPTER 18

COLE

I leaned against the wall outside the restaurant, waiting for my last-minute date to turn up. I had managed to corral up a woman to join me this evening. A friend-with-benefits, a woman with as much a bad reputation as me, one I knew wouldn't turn down a free dinner or make a fuss when I dropped her off without taking her to bed.

Brent and Annette were already inside, but I wasn't going to enter until I had a woman on my arm.

A taxi pulled up and Lola emerged. It'd been a while since I saw her last. She looked good. Her hair was longer and she was dressed in a sexy red dress. I realized she was expecting to get laid.

"Hey," she drawled throatily.

"Hey." I picked myself off the wall and leaned in to give her a kiss on the cheek.

She gave me a funny look as she pulled back. She worked in the same industry as the rest of us and it gave her the whip-smart instincts that everyone had to have to achieve. "What's up?" she asked bluntly.

"Nothing," I denied quickly shaking my head. "You look good."

She smiled confidently. "Tell me something I don't know."

"Come on. Let's go eat," I said, pulling her hand through the crook of my arm. I was dying to get inside and see what was going on with Annette and Brent.

"So, you said there was another couple here?" she murmured.

"Yeah. You know Brent Lawson, right?"

She nodded and looked up at me slyly. "I know his daddy."

"Don't start," I warned.

"Don't worry. I'll play nice."

"So...it's Brent and his date. She's a friend of my sisters, and I thought it would be nice to keep them company."

"And you'll tell me later what this is really about."

I furrowed my brow at her. "You should get out more. You're becoming paranoid."

"Sounds like a terrific evening," she said dryly, as the two of us headed inside.

Annette looked up as soon as I walked in, and a huge smile spread across her face. She rose to her feet and waved to me. "Cole, hi," she greeted, and planted a kiss on my cheek. Enough to pass for familiar, but not so much as to give us away.

Still, I inhaled the scent of her perfume, the smell of her, her closeness, and felt as though I was home again. This was what I'd been missing. The feeling. I moved and introduced Lola to them.

"How lovely to meet you," Lola said, her eyes moving over Annette, the way a snake might over a rat trapped in a corner.

"Good to see you, man." Brent shook my hand and we took our seats.

Lola sat next me and I noticed with some satisfaction that Annette seemed to be eyeing her with an expression I would call jealousy.

We ordered our food and talked about business. We all had plenty of stuff to say about the industry, the work, the silly stories that we had dragged ourselves through in the last couple of months. It seemed to be going along fine until I noticed Brent extending his arm around the back of the booth we were sitting in, and letting his filthy fingers rest on Annette's shoulder.

She didn't seem that bothered by it. Not reacting to his touch, but not pulling away either.

"So, how long have you lived in the city?" Lola asked Annette as our appetizers were cleared away.

"Oh, just since college," Annette replied. "But I like it here. Better than living in the middle of nowhere, that's for sure."

"Yeah, I get that." Brent looked at her with interest.

I knew what he was doing. The prick was being charming.

She flashed him a brief smile, but it seemed a little strained.

"And how did you guys meet?" Annette nodded to the two of us.

Lola glanced at me, probably looking for direction given that the two of us had basically met and started hooking up after running into each other at a club. Not exactly the classiest introduction.

"Uh, through work," I replied quickly.

Lola raised an eyebrow, but didn't confirm or deny my statement.

"Right." Annette nodded, but it was clear she wasn't buying it. She got to her feet and glanced at Lola. "You want to come to the powder room?"

Lola was no fool. "Sure, I could use a touch-up." She patted my shoulder as she slid past me and headed towards the Ladies room.

Now that Brent and I were alone together, I didn't intend to miss the chance to get under his skin. "So, how's it going with you guys?" I asked hurriedly, knowing that my time was limited.

"Uh, fine, I guess." He shrugged. "We met for a coffee earlier in the week. She seems really nice. I think we're on to something."

"Yeah, I don't know about that." I shook my head.

"What do you mean?" he asked, furrowing his brow. "You were the one who introduced us."

"Yeah, as I understand it, she's not really looking for anything serious," I replied. I knew I was being an asshole, but I couldn't stop myself. I wanted Annette for myself, not to give her up to someone as sensationally bland as Brent.

"I don't know about that." He shrugged again. "She seems like she's up for something more serious, based on the conversations we've had."

"Yeah, but—"

"And honestly, I think I'm ready to settle down," he admitted earnestly.

"Really?" I asked dumbfounded by the idiocy of someone wanting to settle down with a woman they had only met once.

He nodded. "Yeah, I mean, I know you like playing the field and all, but it's never really been my thing. I'm ready to really settle down with someone, you know? Especially, someone who's already in the business. That makes sense to me."

"Early days to be thinking of that, surely," I tried to sway his thinking. I was swiftly realizing why this was the most in-depth conversation I had ever managed with Brent before. I would have to struggle to think of anyone I knew who was quite as dull as him.

"Yeah, sure, but I really like her so far," he insisted, and he sounded a little pissed at my attitude.

No wonder too. I had just crashed his first real date with the woman which by all accounts, he was seriously into already.

Before we could continue, the women returned from the bathroom, and I noticed that they weren't speaking to one another.

Annette, especially, seemed distracted by something. She took the seat next to mine.

Lola paused, standing over her. "Uh...?"

Annette looked over at me, then at Brent, and then seemed to realize the mistake she had made and swiftly got to her feet. "I'm sorry." She shook her head, her face bright red. "Guess I'm not thinking straight."

I couldn't help but feel a little internal ping of triumph as she went to take her place next to Brent. She didn't look up at me, but she didn't have to. Because she might not have thought she was thinking straight, but I knew she was. She had naturally been drawn to my side all over again. Deep in her subconscious, she still wanted me. I just had to figure out some way to bring that up to the surface.

CHAPTER 19

ANNETTE

"Hey, girl, I've been thinking a lot about you," Collette said in my ear as soon as I picked up the phone.

"You have?"

"Yeah. I've been feeling bad about what happened between you and Cole.

"Forget about it. It's cool. I'm seeing Brent now." I changed the subject. "I assume marriage is treating you well?"

"Sure is," she replied heartily.

I laughed. I could tell she would be filling me in on all the juicy details as soon as she got the chance.

"I thought we could go for our spa trip soon."

I grinned and leaned back on the couch. We had made a standing spa date a couple of years ago, when the two of us had realized we were making enough money to actually treat ourselves once in a while. It was one of my favorite times of the month, an adventure where we slipped off together, sneaking out for cocktails after our facials, and catching up on all the gossip.

"Yeah, you were pretty shitty throwing off our schedule with your wedding like that," I teased.

She laughed. "So, when are you free?"

"I think I'm free this weekend."

"Nah, not this weekend," she replied. "I'm on my period. I'm going to be home with my feet up marathoning some shitty show, I think."

"Sounds fun." I smiled. "Next weekend?"

"Yeah, that sounds good."

"It's settled then," I agreed.

She fell silent for a moment and I knew what she was thinking. She was wondering, even if she wouldn't come out and say it out loud, what the hell was going on with my personal life.

Truth was, I had no fucking idea, and I didn't want to involve anyone else in it. "Listen, I have to run, but I'll call you tomorrow or something, okay?"

"Okay."

"Bye sweetie," I finished up quickly, and tossed the phone to the other end of the couch. I had done a decent job avoiding Collette, but I hadn't been able to pull off a similar trick with her brother.

It had started with that double-date, where Cole had brought that woman along with him. I had no idea what their relationship truly was, but I had a feeling he wanted it that way. I really think he wanted to keep me guessing, wondering, asking, trying to put the pieces together and figure it out. I had been distracted the entire date, unable to pay attention to Brent the way I wanted to. Or maybe it was just that Brent did very little to excite me. I hadn't gone beyond a kiss with Brent. Plus, I had no real urge to, if I was being honest. He wasn't a bad guy, far from it, but he was on the boring side and a touch too forward when it came to putting his hands all over me.

Nothing like Cole.

Yes, this was what I couldn't shake. Cole would never have pushed to touch me when I didn't want it. That I found conversation between us flowed smoothly and happily, for hours on end. I had taken for granted how easy I found him to talk to, but with Brent, I found that reality thrown into sharp relief, our exchanges were stilted, nervous and laced with second-guessing.

But I'd already made my choice. And it was a good choice. A rational, thinking woman's choice.

I couldn't end up with someone like Cole. If he thought he could do the same kind of thing he had with Lola, with me, he had another thing coming. I wasn't going to be his fuck buddy for all the tea in China.

Even Collette, his own sister had said he was a womanizer.

So there was no point chasing down someone who wouldn't commit to me. Even the night of the date, he had called me up because he'd wanted to set me up with some other friends of his, not to ask me out on a date of our own. He wasn't interested in me for something serious.

I wished now I had not cut Collette off and talked to her instead. Now I would have to wait until next week before I got a chance to do that. Damn her period for coming early.

Furrowing my brow, I crunched some numbers. Hmm... That's strange. Had her period come early? Our cycles were usually pretty well matched, but I hadn't felt so much as a twinge in my belly the last few days. I checked the date. Yeah, she wasn't early. I was late.

I was late.

The horror hit me with the force of a speeding truck. The whole room swayed dangerously. Jesus! I gripped the side of the couch, feeling as though I would fall over, even though I was already lying down. I tried to quell the panic rising in my throat. We'd used a condom every single time. We were so careful.

I didn't have to be pregnant, did I? I could just be late. These things happened. Even if I had been relentlessly timely with my twenty-eight-day cycle for the last ten years.

I found myself suddenly to my feet, making my way to the drugstore down the block from me, my legs moving, moving and my mind whirling. I tried to talk myself out of the swell of panic beating in my brain, begging myself to calm down, to ignore the urge to panic because there was nothing yet to panic about. But I suppose, in the back of my mind, I felt as though I knew something was off. Something serious. Something I wouldn't be able to hide from when I found out the truth.

I picked up a pregnancy test, headed back home, and scrambled into the bathroom.

Please, please, don't let me be pregnant. I had no idea what I would do if I discovered I was carrying Cole's baby. My hands were trembling as I tore off the packaging. I took the test and counted down, second by second, as the time passed, praying to God that it wouldn't be what I thought it was. What I already knew it was.

I opened my eyes slowly as my internal countdown dwindled to nothing, and stared at the test in front of me.

Pregnant.

I dropped my head into my hands, sinking to the floor of the bathroom, focusing on the feeling of the cold tiles on my skin, not allowing the full horror to overcome me.

How could this be? We had always been so, so careful. Had one of them broken? Just plain not worked? I ran through all those warnings I had read about on social media, all the ones that warned women to be careful when they had sex with a condom, because they weren't infallible.

Somehow, I had never imagined in a million years, it would happen to me.

I lay my head on the ground below me, breathing hard. Then I moved my hands down to my belly, wondering if this kid could feel my panic and be born with some kind of complex. How much could fetuses understand? Could it somehow feel that I was freaking the fuck out? I scolded myself internally for cursing in front of the kid, and, suddenly found myself laughing at my ridiculousness.

I peeled myself from the bathroom floor and looked at myself in the mirror.

"Jesus, Annette. You are going to be a mother," my reflection whispered.

No matter what, I had to deal with this. I was an adult and that meant taking responsibility for the choices I had made. Even if those choices had led to me getting knocked up by the last man in the world I wanted to be knocked up by. I lifted my chin and squared my shoulders. No matter what happened, I could do this.

And then I crumpled to the ground again. Maybe I could do it tomorrow.

After I freak the hell out today.

CHAPTER 20

"Annette?"

"Hmmm?"

I looked up from the tiny spot I had been staring at, the single dark dot on the crisp white tablecloth. I couldn't help but think of it as my baby, in a way. A little mark, the kind that you wouldn't even notice until someone told you about it. And when you spotted it, you could never again un-see it. That was all you could see, all you could focus on.

"Are you all right?" Brent asked, eyeing me from across the table.

I supposed I wasn't doing as good a job as I might have hoped, keeping my discomfort in while we ate dinner together. He had texted me not long after the pregnancy test and invited me out to dinner, and I agreed. Anything to get me out of the mess that was my head for a little while. But now that I was here, I wished I could have reeled back time and said no, because I needed to be alone, to process my future, not try to entertain Brent.

"Yeah, I'm fine," I smiled at him.

He reached across the table and took my hand. "You sure I can't get you a drink?"

I shrugged and shook my head. "No, I'm feeling a little under the weather," I said. "Don't want to make it worse..."

"Oh, okay." He nodded, smiling hopefully at me from across the table.

It was our third date, if you counted the coffee he had taken me out for the week before, and I knew what he had to be thinking. But I knew for damn sure there was more chance of the restaurant caving in on us than there was of me going home with him this evening. I couldn't think of anything worse right now. There was a little seed in my body, a new addition that I was still trying to wrap my head around. I ignored the way he stroked his thumb over my knuckles and realized I would have to tell him about the baby. No man would want a woman pregnant with another man's child.

"Shit," Brent muttered suddenly, looking behind me.

I turned to see what had caught his attention, and my heart stopped when I saw Cole making his way towards us. "What the hell is he doing here?" I asked Brent. "Did you mention that we were coming to this place tonight?"

"Yeah, but I didn't think he would actually turn up," he muttered, clearly annoyed. Then he plastered a big smile on his face as Cole approached us.

I shifted in my seat, trying to keep a straight face. Cole knew me well enough to be able to see straight through me if he wanted to, and the last thing I needed was to have him guess that I was carrying his baby. Of course, I would eventually have to tell him, but I figured it would probably be one of the worst things that could happen while you were on a date with another man. I had no intention of putting the theory to the test one way or the other.

"Cole." Brent got to his feet and extended his hand towards his colleague. "Good to see you here. You didn't mention that you'd be coming here this evening."

"I was passing by and I thought I'd come in and say hello."

"Are you planning on dining?" he asked Cole.

"Well, if you guys don't mind me joining you," he said shamelessly, while glancing over at me meaningfully.

"I'll go see if we can get a table for the three of us." Brent stood up, and rolled his eyes at me.

Cole just stood there and watched him walk away.

"What the hell are you doing here?" I demanded, glaring up at him.

"Oh, so you're saying I haven't just made this night a whole lot more interesting?" he asked, his eyes flicking down at me.

Truth was, he had, but I wouldn't give him the satisfaction of knowing this. "You need to get out of here," I muttered aggressively. "You need to go. I can't be around you right now."

"I don't think that's how your date feels," he remarked, as Brent spoke with a waiter.

We were led away to a bigger table and Cole made sure to sit right next to me, grazing his fingers over the exposed skin of my thigh as he did so…. a gesture that could almost be

130

written off as coincidence, but I knew it wasn't. I hated that my body still reacted to his touch. I told myself it was just a learned response. I could very easily unlearn it.

"So, this must be your third date, huh?" Cole remarked as Brent took his seat opposite me.

Brent's jaw tightened, but he nodded. "Yeah, that's right," he replied as he reached over and took my hand again, as though he was proving a point to anyone who cared to glance over at the three of us that it was Brent and I who were on a date, and Cole who was the third wheel. At least, that's what Brent wanted to believe.

"Just a scotch on the rocks, thanks," Cole said to the waiter.

I wondered if he had already been drinking before he had made his way down here. It would explain why he seemed so brazenly unabashed about joining us.

"A glass of still mineral water for my date and a Scotch on the rocks for me please," Brent ordered.

"You not drinking tonight, Annette?" Cole asked, raising his eyebrows.

"No, she's not," Brent jumped in, before I had a chance to answer for myself.

I shifted in my seat, annoyed that he felt the urge to speak for me. I had a mouth, I could use it. Though what I intended to use it for was probably far removed from what he was hoping I would do.

"She's not feeling well tonight," Brent continued, almost proudly, as though he was making a point about how much better he knew me than Cole did.

Cole shifted his leg closer to me, pressing it against mine, and I let it rest there. It felt good, better than I wanted it to.

"Oh, I'm sorry to hear that." Cole looked over at me with genuine concern in his eyes, or what looked like genuine concern.

I had no idea whether it was a game he was playing to make a point about the connection the two of us had, or if it was real anymore.

The food arrived, giving me a good excuse to draw my attention away from his face.

Brent tightened his grip on my hand and didn't release it even as I went to pick up my cutlery. "Brent." I tapped my foot against his beneath the table. "You need to let go of me?"

"Hmm. Right, sure, Of course." He dropped my hand, but he was staring hard at Cole the entire time, as though he was worried the lack of physical contact between us would give his rival a chance to strike.

We ate and I managed to keep the conversation flowing between us. The funny thing was the ridiculous atmosphere between the three of us was finally enough to get my mind off the baby growing in my belly.

The waiter came to clear our plates away. None of us had done justice to our meal.

Brent got to his feet. "I'm going to the bathroom," he announced slowly, looking directly at me, as though he was giving me a chance to interrupt and ask him to stay.

I didn't want him to. I needed to get Cole alone, to figure out what the fuck was happening with us.

As Brent moved past us, Cole slid his hand on to my thigh.

I could have pulled it away, but I didn't. I didn't want to. "I don't know what you're playing at," I told him quickly. "But you—"

Before I could get another word out, he leaned towards me and tried to plant a kiss on my lips.

I managed to pull back before he landed one on me, my squeak of surprise drawing the attention of a few of the other patrons sitting around us. "Okay, you need to settle down," I warned him, lifting my finger and holding him back. My heart was pounding. I wanted nothing more than for him to actually kiss me, to feel his mouth on mine again, to get lost in his embrace. But I couldn't. I was out on a date with another man, for goodness sake. I had decency to think of here. I wasn't an asshole, no matter what my instincts were urging me to do.

"I miss you. So much. I want—"

But before he could go on, Brent returned to the table. He slid down into the seat opposite us, and glanced between us as though he could tell something was amiss. "Everything okay?"

I nodded at once. "Everything's fine," I replied hurriedly, feeling Cole itching to say something next to me. In a perfect world, I would have just told Brent the truth, gotten up and walked out of there with the man I wanted to be with, but this wasn't a perfect world. This was a world where my nana wasn't going to be around for much longer, and I couldn't be wasting my time on a playboy who had decided to play some kind of game. I had to find someone who was going to be a worthy father to my baby.

Oh my God, that was the first time I had thought of the little life growing inside me as mine. *My baby.*

"Can I get you anything else?" the waiter appeared beside us and glanced between the three of us, apparently sensing the atmosphere festering away between us.

"I could use another drink," Brent replied, lifting his glass up.

"And same goes for me." Cole nodded. He glanced in my direction. "Annette? Sure you don't want something?"

"I'm sure," I replied firmly.

He cocked an eyebrow at me.

"Why is that so surprising?" I asked defensively.

"Yeah, why's that so surprising?" Brent echoed.

Cole glanced over at him.

To my horror, I saw something snap within him. Whatever part of him had been playing the dutiful third wheel had run out of patience just like that, and I knew I was in trouble. We all were. There was no way to let Brent down gently.

"Because if I know Annette, I know she likes to drink when she has fun," Cole said. "Though maybe you weren't intending on having any *fun* with Brent?"

I glared at him. I had never been more furious at anyone in my life. I would have leaned over and slapped him, but I knew that what I was going to come out with would hit him that much harder than a blow ever would. "You want to know why I'm not drinking?" I shot back, getting to my feet, my voice shaking with fury.

Cole stared at me, a strange expression on his face, as though he knew he had taken things a step too far.

"I thought it was because you were ill," Brent cut in, confused.

I ignored him. I looked straight at Cole, giving myself one more moment to talk myself out of this if I wanted to. But I didn't. He had to find out sooner or later, didn't he? And it might as well be now. "I'm pregnant," I stated clearly.

The shock on his face was priceless.

No one moved.

"I'm sorry, Brent and thank you so much for the meal." Then I grabbed my coat and headed for the door. I wasn't sticking around to see what happened now. I was hitting the bricks and hoping to God I had made the right decision in telling him. Because I had a strong feeling, I had just made the biggest mistake of my life.

CHAPTER 21

COLE

B rent was sitting there, opposite me, looking as though someone had just punched him in the mouth. And trust me when I say I knew precisely how he was feeling. I felt as though I had been punched in the gut. I got to my feet in a daze, intending to go after Annette before she made it out of the restaurant.

"She's already gone," Brent told me, his tone shaky, as though he too, was trying to wrap his head around what we had just found out.

"I could get out there, make sure she's—"

"She wants to be alone right now," Brent told me firmly. "Come on, dude, you know I'm right—"

"Don't dude me," I shot back, but my knees gave out and I sank back into my seat. I had to change my strategy. Find another way to win her. I cast another look outside onto the street. The thought of Annette out there alone and pregnant made my chest hurt. How could it be that her being pregnant with another man's child didn't do anything to deter me? In

136

fact, I felt even more protective of her than I had been before.

"Well, I guess that's that over with," Brent said, leaning back in his seat. He looked almost amused.

How could he act like this? The woman he was dating, the woman he was sleeping with, had just told him she was pregnant. I'd always known that he had an element of asshole in there, but this was beyond anything that I had ever seen from him before. "You're really just going to let her walk out of here?" I demanded.

"What are you talking about?" Brent rolled his eyes. "She's not my problem. I mean, it's a shame, I thought we were getting on pretty well, but still. Let's not overstate this. I'm not getting stuck with something like that."

"Are you serious right now?" I exploded. All the booze I had consumed all day and the shock rushing through my system was making a mess of my thoughts, a mess so confusing I couldn't make sense of it. Buried in there somewhere too was this hint of jealousy, knowing that she let him in where I had been kept out.

"Hey, keep your voice down. You're drunk, aren't you?" Brent snapped. "No need to make more of a scene than you already have."

"No, you look me in the face and tell me you don't care about that woman," I demanded belligerently. I couldn't think straight anymore. Why was I pushing him towards her? I wanted her. I was supposed to be dissuading him.

"I don't." He looked confused, meeting my gaze.

The swell of anger took me over. I didn't know what I was

doing as I reached across to him, grabbed his collar, and pulled him across the table towards me. The plates slid across the table dangerously and smashed on the ground.

The waiter, returning with our drinks, froze on the spot in shock.

The entire restaurant had turned their attention to us, and I was distinctly aware of all the eyes on me. But I didn't care. This fucker got my girl pregnant. "You bastard," I roared furiously.

He yanked himself away from me, but before he could catch himself, he went tumbling backwards, pulling the tablecloth off the table, sending all plates and glasses crashing down around us. He glared at me as he scrambled to his feet. "I don't know why you're talking like I have to be the one to step up," he snarled at me. "I'm not the one who knocked her up. We've never even slept together!"

I blinked at him, my mind blank and foggy.

Brent pulled out his wallet and tossed a few hundred down on the table. "That should cover the damage," he snapped, dusting off his jacket and his shirt. "I'll be sending you the bill for the dry-cleaning, Cole." Then he stormed out of the restaurant.

The waiter came to grab the money, not looking me in the eye, probably worried I would take a swing at him.

I didn't move. If Brent wasn't the father…

I ran out to the street and inhaled a huge lungful of air, hoping the crisp coolness would be enough to give me clarity. Brent was just collateral damage, an unfortunate bystander.

The baby was mine.

Sweet Lord, Annette was pregnant with my child.

I began to laugh with joy. It was like a fountain inside me. It bubbled out and made me shake with laughter. A couple was passing and I grabbed the man's hand. He thought I was a drunk and tried to shake me off.

"I'm going to be a father," I shouted.

"Congratulations," the woman said with a laugh.

"Yeah, congratulations. I'm very happy for you," the man said, patting me on the back.

"I going to be a father!" I shouted again.

I tipped my head back and closed my eyes, letting the cool evening air rush over me. I had to get to her. I had to get to Annette and tell her I understood. That I would be there for her. I would help her raise the baby. I would do anything she needed me to. Even if it meant turning my entire life upside down, it would be worth it. As long as I got to be with her.

Now, I just had to figure out where the hell she went.

CHAPTER 22

As I made my way through the city, I struggled to think straight. Had I really just done that? Told Cole about the baby over dinner with another man? It was crazy. Stupid. Vindictive. I should have waited, should have held out, but there was some part of me that needed him to know, needed the weight of this to be spread between the two of us.

I couldn't carry it alone. It was his baby too.

I'll apologize to Brent tomorrow. I wasn't even sure where I was going, until I found myself on the train out of the city, headed towards Nana's place. I knew that the stress of all of this was probably the last thing she needed right now, but I had to see her. I needed to talk to someone who understood me, someone who could take care of me, somebody who could help me make sense of my life. I wanted to curl up on my nana's couch and forget all of this had ever happened. For her to make it all better for me, even though I was an adult and I should have been handling this all by myself.

I collapsed into a seat on the train, feeling as though the weight of the world was bearing down on top of me. I stared out of the train window. My face reflected in the glass, I looked pale and sad. But I wasn't sad. Not really. I was strong and I would survive. Me and my baby. We'd work it out somehow.

As I eased myself off the train, I was already desperate for the bathroom. I guessed I had better get used to it. This was probably what it would be like all the time while I was pregnant. Maybe I should take another test and make sure? Maybe this was all just some faulty drugstore brand cheapness, and I could remedy it by checking again.

But I knew in my heart what the truth was.

My period was late, I was bloated, my boobs hurt. I was as pregnant as they come. I just wanted to find a way out of the fact that I had somehow allowed myself to get pregnant by the one man in this city I had sworn I would never have anything more than pure fun with.

I was willing to bet he wasn't too happy with my announcement. After all, he had let me walk out of that place without trying to stop me. Yeah, there was more than a small part of me mad at him for that too. Why hadn't he chased after me, taken care of me?

Selfish bastard.

How could he not see that I needed him now? It wasn't like I expected him to come howling out after me into the street, but maybe, just maybe, he could have called me on my phone by now. I didn't even need him to take care of me and the baby, just an acknowledgement would have been nice. It would make me feel like he hadn't used me and abandoned me.

Before I knew it, I was out in the street once more, and striding purposefully towards my nana's place. I had only seen her three times since the wedding. Mainly because she always claimed she was too tired to see me. And I was fearful about what looking her in the eye might do to me. Now I had news to share with her that would change everything. I didn't have a man, but I was going to have a baby.

I hesitated before I knocked on her door. Did I really want to burden her with all of this? She was already going through so much already, and I wasn't sure if I could dump this on her as well. Then I decided she had to know. Who knows, maybe the doctors were wrong? Maybe she'd live long enough to see her grandchild being born. The thought made me feel happy.

I knocked on the door and heard some movement inside. I tried my best to prepare myself for what she might look like. The last two trips here she'd been in bed looking pale and listless while all she wanted to talk about was whether I had found someone. I had no idea how far the disease might have inched up inside of her, I had to be ready to lay eyes on her and see the devastation. I closed my eyes, took a deep breath, and made a big attempt at getting my emotions in check.

She opened the door.

I opened my eyes and looked at her. The light was behind her and I couldn't see her face properly.

She could see me though and she knew at once something was wrong. Instantly, she leaned forward and wrapped her arms around me. "Oh, baby," she cooed in my ear. "There, there, what's wrong? Come inside, let me get you a nice cup of hot chocolate..."

"I messed up, Nana," I blurted, as tears burned the backs of my eyes. "I'm so sorry. I didn't mean to…"

"What happened?" she asked, grabbing my arm and leading me through to the kitchen. She seemed spritely enough, but then perhaps she had just had a rush of energy when she saw me, knowing that I needed taking care of.

"I don't even know how to tell you..." I trailed off, sinking down on a seat in the kitchen.

She stroked my head. "Don't say a thing. Just catch your breath while I make you a drink first."

I watched her as she moved about making us a pot of hot chocolate. I realized suddenly she was avoiding my gaze, as though she worried that she'd give something away by looking into my eyes. And another thing I realized too. She looked really healthy. Nothing like the pale, weak figure of my last two trips. A sudden thought hit me. They say that people always seem to revive and look their best just before they die.

"Nana," I said carefully. "How is your health?"

She stopped pottering around and turned around to face me. "Annette, there's something I have to tell you." Her voice wavered slightly.

My eyes widened. "What is it?" I demanded. "What's wrong? Are you okay? Is it to do with the...with your illness?"

"Yes, I suppose so," she conceded. She walked up to the kitchen table and sank down into the seat opposite me. "Annette, I...I feel so terrible about this. I just can't keep it in for another second."

"What's wrong?" I whispered.

She flicked her gaze back and forth between my eyes for a moment before she replied. "I'm not dying."

It took me a moment to figure out what the hell she was talking about. I had spent so long hoping to hear those words out of her mouth that now, I couldn't make sense of it. "What do you mean? What are you talking about? Are you cured?"

"I know I shouldn't have said it," she continued, talking quickly, the words tumbling from her before she could stop them. "I had a few drinks, and being around Collette and with her getting married, I couldn't help but think. Well, what happens when I really am gone and there's no-one left to take care of you. I just wanted you to be happy. I just wanted you to have someone, the same way—"

"Nana, stop," I ordered, holding my hand up to silence her in the middle of her rant. "You need to stop because I don't understand a word you're saying."

"I'm not sick. I was never sick."

I shook my head to clear it. "So you're not dying?"

"No more than we all are, all the time," she replied, with the flicker of a smile.

"You were pretending to lie in bed and look sick the last two times."

"Sorry."

"You lied to me?" I exclaimed incredulously. I almost couldn't believe what she'd just said.

"Well—?" she began.

"I can't believe you would do this to me," I muttered. "You pretended to be dying just because you wanted to hurry me to the altar?"

"Because I knew you deserved someone," she corrected.

I shook my head again. "No, you don't get to…" I rubbed my hand over my face. This didn't make any fucking sense.

"Forget about me. What was it you wanted to tell me?" she asked.

In the shock of her news, I had forgotten the most pressing matter at hand. That I was pregnant— I was fucking pregnant, a consequence of the lie she had dumped on my doorstep. I figured there was no point holding back any longer. "I'm pregnant," I told her, letting the words hang with a punishing severity in the air between us.

"You're pregnant?" Her bright blue eyes practically bulged out of her head. "Are you serious?"

I nodded.

"How far along are you? Who's the father? Are you going to keep it?"

"I'm only a few weeks in right now and yes, I'm keeping it," I admitted.

"And the father? Who is he? Tell me," she demanded, grasping my hand and squeezing hard. "I can't believe this is really happening. After all this time..."

"The father is Cole," I replied. I felt raw, torn open, as though there was nothing I could have kept from her even if I'd wanted to.

"Cole?" She furrowed her brow, trying to place the name. "Do I know...?" She trailed off as she remembered exactly where she knew the name from. Her eyes widened. "Collette's brother?" she gasped. I supposed his reputation was wide enough that even she had picked up on it.

"Yeah, Collette's brother." I sighed heavily and ran my hands through my hair. "And he's not exactly...he's not exactly the settling-down type, you know?"

"Yes, I heard about that." She nodded, frowning slightly. My grandmother knowing that gossip would have been funny, if it weren't for the circumstances at hand.

"And I should never..." I shook my head. "I would never have done anything with him, but I was so upset and frightened at the thought of losing you that day at the wedding—and he was there—and he was looking after me, so..."

"Are you guys...together?" she asked, as delicately as she could.

"No," I barked. I put my head into my hands and let out a groan. "Nana, I think I'm in love with him," I mumbled into my fingers.

She fell silent for a long moment, and I knew she was doing

her best to process what I just told her. "You think he would—"

"It's complicated," I cut her off before she could go on any further. "I don't even know if he wants anything to do with the baby. It might interfere with his swinging lifestyle." I felt bitter and lonely.

She reached over and put her hand on my stomach, her fingers pulsing through my skin. Her life, and the life of this baby, connected through me.

I felt tears come to my eyes. All of this had been such a mess, the emotions were just sneaking up on me, taking control. I leaned my head on to her shoulder and let the tears flood down my face.

"He knows?"

"He knows," I replied once I had managed to get my breath back. "At least, I think he does. I only told him...an hour ago."

"Oh, my goodness," she gasped. "And what did he do? What did he say?"

"I left before he could say anything," I admitted. "We took precautions so this shouldn't have happened. It just feels..." I searched for the word, but nothing came up.

"But you do want this baby, right?"

I looked into her searching eyes. Deep inside me, I knew I was excited about this. Yes, there was fear, regret and hurt that Cole might not want to be part of my baby's life. I felt panic and even confusion, but there was great excitement there, too. Because I wanted this baby. Even if he didn't want to raise this kid with me, I would do it alone. With my nana.

Even though I was still mad as hell at her for lying to me in such an outrageous scheme, at least she was going to stick around long enough to help me out. For that, I felt thankful. More than thankful. I would rather she played a thousand tricks on me than lose her.

Suddenly, a knock sounded at the door.

Nana extracted herself from me and got to her feet.

"Are you expecting someone?" I asked.

She shook her head.

CHAPTER 23

ANNETTE

She approached the door slowly, carefully, as though she had no idea who could be knocking on her door at this time of the night. Chewing her lip, she peered through the peephole. When she glanced back over at me, her eyes were wide and her expression was full of drama. "*It's Cole,*" she mouthed.

"Let him in," I said. My heart was pounding. He had followed me here? Or maybe he had guessed where I would be going and gotten Nana's address from Collette. Whatever it was, I didn't know what he would say.

She opened the door.

Cole, looking rattled and disheveled, peered past her into the house. "Annette," he gasped, practically tumbling over the doorstep.

Nana nimbly stepped out of the way to let him by, raising her eyebrows at me as he made his way towards the kitchen.

"You're all right." He planted himself down opposite me and grabbed my hands.

I looked beyond him to my grandmother.

He glanced over his shoulder and suddenly seemed to realize he had just barreled his way into her house with no explanation. He leapt to his feet and extended his hand towards her. "Sorry to barge in like this. I'm Cole. Good to meet you," he introduced himself smoothly.

Nana allowed his big hand to completely envelop hers. "I know who you are young man," she replied sternly, but gave me a little look like *hmmm, he seems nice.*

Yeah that wasn't what I needed right now.

"I'll give you some space," she said before retreating to the living room.

Cole returned his attention to me. "God, I'm so glad you're okay! I've been so worried." He grabbed my hands again, sinking to the ground in front of me, on his knees – as though he was proposing.

I closed my eyes. This was too much, far too much. "Cole, what are you doing here?" I demanded.

He swallowed and took a deep breath. "I couldn't contact you. Either your battery is dead or you switched off your phone. I had to call Collette and it wasn't pretty."

"Cole, what are you doing here?" I repeated.

He ran his hand through his hair, making it even more disheveled and beautiful than it already was.

God, I was such a sucker for this man.

"Annette, I want to be with you," he confessed. "I know...I know that I was a fuck-up at the start. I should have told you from that first night that I actually felt something for you."

"But you didn't," I reminded him. "You just told me – you just told me you wanted me before I got all settled down. You wanted a piece of me before you couldn't any more. That's what you said, remember?"

"Of course, I remember." He winced at the memory of it. "But that's not what I should have done. I should have just been honest and told you that I wanted you, but I had no idea how the hell I was meant to come out with that. I had my pride too. You were Collette's best friend and you seemed only to want a short fling with me. The only thing I could think of was introducing you to my friends. It seemed to work."

"Yeah, well, for future reference, setting me up with your friends isn't really the best way to show interest," I shot back, a quiver in my voice.

"I wasn't actually going to go through with it. I wanted you for myself. And for your information, Brent is not even really my friend. I couldn't believe it when he called my name at the airport. I wanted to punch his head in when he took your number," he explained. "And if I'd just been able to come out and tell you the fucking truth about how I felt, then none of this would have happened. And that's my fault, and I'm sorry. But now that you're pregnant—"

"Now that I'm pregnant, what?" I demanded, and I was shocked to find the anger pulsing through my system at what he was suggesting. "Now you've decided that nobody else can have me, right?"

"Pretty much," he replied, a smug smile curling up the corners of his mouth.

I wanted to grab his face and kiss him, yet strangle him at the same time. Because he needed to know he'd really made me suffer. "That's not how it works," I shot back. "You don't get to just undo it all like that. You don't get to go from setting me up with your co-workers to coming here and saying you want to be with me."

"I know I fucked up, Annette, trust me, I do," he admitted, he suddenly looked crestfallen. "But I just want you to give me a chance—"

"You had so many chances before this," I reminded him, getting to my feet and crossing my arms over my chest.

"I know I did, I know." He stood up and clasped my arms, looking right into my eyes. "And I'm just asking for one more chance, that's all."

"I don't know what to think or feel right now. This all has bee— with you and now, the baby and my nana. I need time." I pointed towards the door. "So I need you to just walk out of here and give me some space to think about everything."

"You really want me to go?" he asked.

I nodded. "Yeah, I think you should," I replied, my voice tight and small.

"Annette, please—"

"Excuse me, Cole." My grandmother slid back into the room, and took his arm. "I think my granddaughter has made herself clear. Maybe you should listen to her."

"Are you sure this is what you want?" Cole turned to me.

I nodded.

Half of me wanted him to stay, but I knew that it was the best choice for him to go. I needed time to think. We both did. All of this was a lot to take in and both of us needed some time to figure this out.

Cole let out a long, reluctant sigh, clearly not wanting to go, but he headed to the door anyway. He shot me one last despairing look as he stood in the doorway, and then stepped out on to the cold street outside.

I sank back into the chair and pressed my lips together. I felt as though I wanted to cry, even though I was too exhausted to muster up so much as a tear.

Nana took a seat next to me and squeezed my shoulder. "It's going to be all right, baby," she cooed.

I had no idea whether she was talking to me or the baby I was carrying in my belly. I put my hands on my stomach and tried to feel it, wondering if it could tell it's father had just been here. Being no more than a cluster of cells at the moment, I shouldn't have been getting so attached to it already, but I was.

"Is it?" I turned to her, too exhausted to believe that things were going to get any better than this. How could they? I wanted Cole back and I wanted him gone at the same time. I felt as though I was losing my mind, going a little crazy with the mess we had made of all of this.

"Maybe you should give it some time," she suggested gently.

I got to my feet, and headed for the stairs. "I'm going to wash up. And then get some sleep. I can think about this in the morning."

As I ascended the stairs, I turned around and looked at Nana. I smiled. "I'm really glad you're not dying, Nana. Please don't ever do that to me again."

Her hands were clasped in front of her. "I'll never do that again," she promised.

I nodded and carried on up the stairs. As I reached the top, I took my phone out of my purse and looked at it. Cole was right. I must have accidentally switched it off. I switched it on again and my phone buzzed in my pocket. I was all ready to ignore the call from Cole or remind him that I needed some time, but it was Collette. I answered the call, not really sure what to expect. "Collette?"

"Annette. Oh, thank God. Are you all right?" she demanded.

"Yeah, yeah, I'm fine," I assured her. "Why? What's going on?"

"Cole called me," she confessed. "He sounded…fuck, Annette, he sounded really cut-up. I don't think I've ever heard him like that before."

"What do you mean?"

"Honestly, I couldn't believe what a state he was in," she continued. "But he was blurting it all out in such a mess I could hardly make sense of it. But eventually, I figured it was about you, and I guessed that you would be the best person to talk to about what the hell is actually happening with the two of you. Is everything okay?" She fell silent.

I realized she was waiting for me to fill in the blanks of the rest of the story. I had no idea where to begin. How much did she even know? How much did Cole want her to know? There was a chance I was about to drop way more information than she needed to hear on her lap. I didn't want to do that, not one little bit. I needed to stay focused on the task at hand, on keeping my personal shit together. But knowing Cole had been upset enough to call his sister in distress...

"I don't know what's happening with us," I admitted. "I mean, this night, it's been...a lot."

"Look, when you told me that you had feelings for my brother, I thought you were crazy," she told me in her usual blunt fashion. "I thought that he was just stringing you along like he had with all the other women in his life. But the way he spoke about you tonight, Annette, it wasn't just like him at all. I think he's really fallen for you..." She trailed off.

She didn't need to fill in the blanks of the rest of the statement for me. It wasn't just sex. It had never been just sex, not with us. I had known that, for a long time. Still, everything he had put me through, was it really worth it? He was a player at heart, and I wasn't sure that a player could ever really stop playing the game he'd spent so long perfecting.

"Collette, the way my brother sounded on the phone," she continued. "He was miserable. I don't think I've ever heard him that miserable in all his life. And I don't want to come storming in there and tell you how you should live your life, but if there are feelings there, I don't think you should abandon them just yet, you know?"

"You were the one who told me to forget about him," I reminded her.

She sighed over the line. "Yeah, I did, but I thought I was doing you a favor. But now I can see – hell, now I can see that my brother is actually stuck on someone, and that someone just happens to be my best friend."

I fell silent. When she put it like that, it felt a bit exhilarating.

"Just...think about it, okay?" She pleaded.

"I will," I promised her. "Look, Collette, I have to go. I need to get some rest..."

"You do that," she agreed. "I'll speak to you soon, all right?"

"Okay," I replied. "Goodnight."

"Night."

I hung up the phone and headed through to the bathroom. I splashed some cold water on my face and gazed at myself in the mirror. My eyes were glittering. Well, at least Nana wasn't going anywhere too soon. I had the baby and Cole cared for me for the time being. Maybe I could make the pieces fit.

Or maybe, when it came to stuff like this, things wouldn't fit so neatly. Cole could father our child even if he couldn't commit completely. Getting my heart broken just scared me silly, so maybe I could keep him just in the co-parent role. There were so many jagged edges and pieces between us and all kinds of stuff getting in the way. Maybe I could wait and see if he was really serious about us? Or if his notion to be a one-woman guy would wear off soon. I needed to see it last for a bit to believe it I suppose.

CHAPTER 24

COLE

I'd tried so hard, every way I could think of, and nothing had worked, and now I was down to the wire and I knew I had to pull this off if I had any chance of actually being with the woman I loved.

Yeah, loved.

Such a weird thought for me, even though I knew it was true. As soon as I found out about the baby, something clicked into place in my mind, something I had been trying to ignore ever since the first night with Annette—we were meant to be together, always had been, and always would be. I had been dumb enough to need a baby to see that, but now that I had, I would make this happen. I was a man of my word, and I knew how to close a deal. And this would be the deal of my life if I could finally get it to stick.

I had enlisted pretty much everyone in on my quest to prove to Annette that I was the right man for the job. My sister, her grandmother, everyone I could find who had a direct line to her, but Annette was still holding back, and if I were being honest, I didn't totally blame her. I'd fucked her around big-time with all the shit I had pulled, and if I were her, facing such an enormous life change, I would have been reluctant to allow someone like me in on it as well.

So I just needed to get her to see that I was the man for this job. I wasn't that shallow playboy she imagined I was. I could make this work between us.

Annette and I had talked a little since she had broken the news to me. I had tried to meet with her in person, but she had been reluctant to.

"This is all confusing enough as it is," she said. "I don't want to throw you on top of it and make it even harder to wrap my head around."

"I need to see you," I pleaded.

Then she hung up before I could say another word. I understood she was going through a hard time, but I needed her to know that I would be there for her, that no matter what she might have believed before, I was a changed man from the person I had been before I had met her.

Before her, I'd never imagined I would find anyone who completely fulfilled me the way she did, anyone who made me feel good the way she did. Even now whenever I thought about her, I felt this rush of peace and calm. As though my body was telling me, *her, it's her, it's always been her.*

I enlisted her grandmother in helping me figure out what the best course of action was. I also found out she had lied to Annette about being terminally ill in order to push Annette into finding a man. So no wonder Annette was running around like a headless chicken in her desperation trying to find a good man and settle down. She had to be still pretty fucked-up after thinking her grandmother was dying for a whole month. If any of my family had dared pull a stunt like that, I would never have spoken to them again.

"I'm her only family," Hazel her nana had told me, over a coffee. "She doesn't have anyone else to go to. I did it because I care about her. I want her to have someone of her own."

"But that doesn't mean you can exploit that," I said.

She shook her head. "I know, and if I could take it back, I would. I guess we've both got some making-up to do, right?"

"Yeah, we do," I agreed. "And I think I have an idea of how to do it..."

The two of us put our heads together and conspired to come up with something that would sell the deal to Annette. No, not the deal, I had to stop thinking about it like that. It was a chance for me to share my life with someone, to give myself over to another human, to start a family of my own.

Hell, even being around Hazel was enough to underline just how much I needed Annette, just how much balance she brought to my life. I'd been running so fast and so hard for so long, that stopping sometimes seemed scary, but as long as she was there beside me, I could do it.

So the two of us started working on the project of a lifetime. I knew the life I had built for myself wasn't exactly conducive to opening up to a baby, so this meant I needed to start again from scratch. New apartment, new part of the city, new décor...and most importantly, a nursery.

"Are you sure this is a good idea?" Hazel asked me, as we stepped back to check out the work we'd done so far.

I glanced over at her. "I don't care." I shrugged. "As long as it makes her happy."

"I think she will be," Hazel replied, a small confident smile on her face.

After a couple of weeks, the nursery was complete – Collette came around to help me add the last few touches to the place, knowing what her best friend would like.

When Collette left, I walked around the place on my own. I could hear my own footsteps, the sound of my breathing. The place was ready—waiting for her.

Now I felt even more nervous than I had been before. At least until now, I had a distraction to keep my mind from wandering to the possibility she would say no. Now I had to go ask that question once again.

Which was how I found myself waiting nervously outside her office, counting down the minutes till she came out, knowing Collette was in the process of hurrying her out the door. Annette had no I would be stopping by...already over-thinking every single way she could shoot me down. Maybe she would completely ignore me, walk straight past me. Maybe she would tell me to leave her alone.

Finally, the time came, and the door to her office opened.

My heart pounded in my chest as I saw her for the first time in what felt like forever. I had missed her so much, so much that I could hardly wrap my head around it. I wanted to pull her into my arms, smell her hair, tell her how much I'd missed her. Instead, I stood there, staring at her, watching her eyes as they widened with shock at seeing me again.

"Cole?" she murmured, moving towards me slowly as though she was sure I would flicker out of existence if she moved too fast.

"Yeah, it's me." I took her hand, and noticed she didn't pull back.

She smiled, then looked away from me. "You shouldn't be here," she said softly, like she wasn't even sure she wanted me to hear the words.

"But I am," I pointed out. "And there's a reason for that."

"And what might that me?" She looked at me expectantly.

"I have something I need to show you." I took her hand and tugged her down the street.

"Where are we going?" she asked.

I noticed the fact that she wasn't pulling away from me, or seem too horrified by my attention, as I'd imagined she might be. "You'll see."

"If you're kidnapping me, you're doing a bad job of it," she teased. "Everyone here has seen us together."

"I'm not kidnapping you," I promised. "I just need you for a minute, that's all."

It wasn't long until we had arrived at the apartment I had decked out for her. We paused outside the door, as though she knew stepping over the threshold would be tantamount to accepting something. Even if that something was only the effort I'd put in to prove myself to her.

"Are you ready?" I asked.

She nodded.

I took her hand and she squeezed back. Oh wow, I felt that familiar jolt of happiness at her touch. I wasn't sure I would ever get tired of being around her like this. There'd always been something so good, so pure about having her near me. I opened the door and she stepped inside.

She looked around, her eyes wide as she took it all in. "Cole, what is this?" she asked quietly, turning around to face me.

I smiled at her. "This is yours. For you and the baby. Close to your work, and it's all laid out already, plus I have a cleaning service and a nanny on retainer as backup if you need it..." I trailed off as I saw her face. I couldn't read her expression and I didn't like that. "Annette?" I prompted her, as she made her way slowly around the living room.

"This place is perfect," she breathed, turning to face me. "How did you get it so perfect? I don't understand..."

"Your nana helped me with it," I replied. "And Collette, too. I wanted this place to be perfect for you."

"Just for me?" she asked, furrowing her brow at me.

I wasn't sure what she was asking, even though I hoped I'd gotten her meaning right. "It can be for both of us, if you want." I moved towards her, smiling hopefully. I didn't dare believe this just yet. "I mean, there's space for us both. For all three of us. I would love to share it with you, but even if you don't want me here, this place is still yours, Annette. I just want to know that you and the baby have somewhere safe and good to live."

"Well, I don't think we could have that unless you were here with us," she murmured gently.

It took me a moment to figure out what she was saying, but when she came over to me and wound her arms around my shoulders, I knew what she was telling me. "You want me to live here with you?" I asked.

Annette nodded. "Of course, I do." She leaned up and planted a kiss on my lips. "You think I'm letting you get out of your duties that easily? I don't think so."

I picked her up and swung her around with joy. Then I kissed her properly. I couldn't believe how good it felt to have her here, to be in this place, this home that we were going to share together. With the baby, too.

"Fair warning, though," she continued. "I might just be hormonal, so if you fuck me around one more time..."

"I won't, I promise." I planted a hand on my heart. "Swear to God. I'm in this forever."

"I should hope so." She smiled. "Because I have a baby in my oven, and I can't afford to wait around on some fuckboy who doesn't know what he wants."

"I promise I'm not going to do anything like that," I swore to her. "No more fuckboy."

She grinned and sank into me, pressing her head to my shoulder. "I just wanted a reason to believe you," she murmured, the sound slightly muffled. "I wanted to be with you so badly, Cole, I just didn't want to get hurt. Not on top of having the baby, not with..."

"Trust me, I get it." I hugged her close. "And I know I'm going to have to work hard to prove that I'm not going to hurt you again, but I'll spend every day proving that to you, if I have to."

"You might have to," she teased, pulling back. Her eyes were glistening with tears, but they were happy ones.

It was the first time I'd ever put happy tears on a girl's face, and there was something so sweet about the idea. I wanted to do more of it. "I've got something to show you." I took her hand.

She grinned. "Better than this?"

"Better than this." I nodded, as we headed through to the nursery that Hazel had carefully helped me put together, piece by piece. We had scoured second-hand stores and online auctions until we had come up with the perfect blend of old and new for Annette.

I pushed the door open and she stepped inside.

For a moment, she didn't say anything, as though she was working her hardest to take in what was in front of her. The crib was antique, the changing table minimalist and new – the window on the opposite side of the room filtered pale light over the pastel green and blue of the nursery, picking out the details in the dusky afternoon sunlight. She walked to the rocking horse with the blue saddle that her nana had showed me a picture of. "This is incredible."

Yes! Exactly what I wanted to hear. I walked towards her and wrapped my arms around her waist, hooking my chin over her shoulder. "I'm glad you like it."

"And I know our baby is going to like it, too," she whispered, taking my hands and moving them over her stomach.

Although it was way too early to feel anything in there, I convinced myself that I could feel a kick, a happy, contented, approving little movement from our child in her belly. "This is going to be amazing," I murmured to her.

She nodded. "Yeah, it totally is."

CHAPTER 25

COLE

I closed my eyes, then opened them again. Yes, this was really happening. I looked up at the window above me, at the light coming through the stained glass, reminded of the very first time the two of us had stepped into the nursery together. How long had it been? Six months? It felt like a lifetime, a world away. But it had been the start of everything for us, the start of the journey that we took together.

Now, here we were, on our wedding day, at this old church that Hazel had helped us pick out. She'd been in on the plans from the start, helping me choose a ring for Annette, and a proposal location, calling us right after it had happened, as though she had somehow felt that cosmic tremor as Annette had put the ring on her finger.

Yeah, I took us down to Vegas, back to that hotel room where it had all started. It had been so perfect it had made my heart ache. She said yes without a second thought, leaning down and wrapping her arms around me, peppering kisses all over my face, her belly jutting against me. And the best part....I could feel our baby kicking away happily.

"I don't know if we're going to have time to plan the wedding after the baby's here," she remarked at the dinner I took her to after she had said yes.

"What are you saying?" I asked.

"That we should do it before he comes along," she replied, running her hand over her stomach and flashing me a smile that told me she wasn't going to let this go easily.

I raised my eyebrows. "That soon? We only have a couple of months..."

"I love a challenge," she replied breezily. "If you're up for this, I am, too."

"Then I guess I'm as ready as you are."

And that was that.

Ever since we'd gotten together, my life had improved so much that to look back on what it had been before her felt distant. A dry emotionless desert. She once accused me of proposing to her to give my child a name, but I had proposed because I wanted nothing more than for her to carry my name. And when she suggested we bring it forward? Well, that was just ensuring that our life together got started sooner rather than later.

The wedding planning was hectic as hell, but my sister and Hazel helped out every way they could to make things easier for Annette, thank goodness. I wasn't sure they could bring it together in time, but they actually pulled it off, much to my shock. My sister laughed at me. "It's called money, Cole. It seriously helps the pieces to fall into place." Yeah, I guess my money helped. I was happy to hand it over. Giving the woman of my dreams the wedding of her lifetime made me swell up with pride.

I wanted to give her every last thing I could.

The last few months, though, had been an education. When we had gotten together for real, I had felt as though I was pitching myself off the side of a cliff. I had no idea what to expect. I'd never done anything like this before, let alone jumping straight-up into a relationship, getting married and having a baby all at once. Things could have gone so badly. Hell, I think most people around us expected them to. But they didn't.

She fell off the same cliff as me and we flew together. It was beautiful.

So one month before she was due to have our baby here we were in church. As the music filled the church, I decided to sneak a look over my shoulder at her. And when I did, everything seemed to stop for a moment.

The place wasn't full. We had decided to keep things small, just family and a few close friends, but it might as well have been empty. She was the only person I saw. The air seemed to still around her, dressed all in white, her dress layered with soft lace that hugged every inch of her gorgeous body like it had been made for her. I stared at her in total fascination.

She hadn't let me catch even a glimpse of her before the wedding, but I knew she would look beautiful. She always did, especially now while she was deep into her pregnancy and glowing like there was a light beneath her skin.

Annette took the last few steps up the aisle towards me. I

took her hand, almost reverently. I knew this place was made for worshipping God, but at that moment, I would have happily gotten down on my knees and worshipped her, instead. "You look beautiful," I whispered and leaned in to kiss her. Then I remembered we were meant to hold off for the kiss until we'd actually done the whole ceremony thing.

She smiled at me, her eyes shining with excitement.

"Are you ready to begin?" the priest asked.

I turned to him.

Collette was grinning broadly at me, the happiness leaking over into her as well. She must have been thinking about her own wedding, the day that had brought Annette and me together in the first place.

"Yes, we are." I nodded.

Annette took my hand and held it tight. And with that, the ceremony began.

I had always imagined agreeing to spend my life with another person would be frightening, but with her, every promise I made, every vow I took, it just felt obvious. Of course, it would be like this. Of course, it was going to be forever. There was no question in my mind, no fear, no doubt. No matter our legal status, I intended to spend the rest of my life with this woman, and nothing would change that or take it away from me.

We said our vows in front of all the people who mattered most to us.

Suddenly, I saw her eyes well up and I felt a warmth rush through my body with a feeling I recognized at once. I had never experienced it before I met her. It was the quiet knowledge I was with the person I was meant to be with and what I was doing was right. The universe was aligning so all the pieces could fit into place around me.

As the priest finished up, after we said our "I dos" and exchanged our rings. I wiped her cheeks with my thumbs and looked her in the eyes, waiting for those precious words I'd been holding out for all this time.

"You may kiss the bride."

With tears in my own eyes, I slid my hands around her waist. I knew this was meant to be chaste, but that wasn't true to our marriage now, was it? I leaned forward and kissed her, softly, slowly, deeply, telling her with my body, heart and soul that for every day to come I would love her more, need her even more deeply, and want her even harder than the last.

When I pulled back, she fluttered her eyes open and smiled. "I love you," she murmured.

"I love you too," I whispered.

Across the church, somebody started to clap.

I looked up and saw Hazel leading the applause and soon, the whole room was celebrating our love, our little family, and our future. I knew now that for all the time I'd spent running from something just like this, I had been running towards this moment, towards this kiss, towards her.

CHAPTER 26

EPILOGUE

ANNETTE

"Is he sleeping?" Cole slipped into the room behind me.

I raised my gaze from the beautiful baby boy asleep in the crib before me to the beautiful man above me. I wasn't sure how long I had been standing there just watching him sleep, but I had a habit of getting lost while he was resting. I just loved to see him at peace, his little fists clenched as he dreamed of something I could only begin to imagine. "Yeah, he's asleep," I whispered.

Cole hugged me from behind, placing his hands on the very stomach that had held this perfect little guy for so long. His wedding ring glinted in the morning light. "So, what do you want to do today?" he asked, kissing my neck gently.

I smiled happily. Because I knew exactly what I wanted to do today.

Being parents had been so much more than I ever could have imagined it would be. Don't get me wrong, I knew it would be a hell of a trip. My nana had done her best to warn me about all the ways that bringing a little person into the world would tear my life apart, but I was loving every second.

Sure, his birth had been rough, long, and more than a little scary. But when he popped out into the world, I took him into my arms, looked down at him, and knew instinctively that I was blessed. I'd heard a lot about how mothers fell in love with their children the very first time they laid eyes on them, but I hadn't really believed it until that moment. I thought it would be like any other relationship. I would grow to love him as I learned his personality, but it was an instant thing with Thomas.

I adored him from the second I saw him. And so did his father.

After the shotgun wedding, we had finished doing up the apartment, filling it with the last few bits and pieces we would need to sustain our life together, and then Thomas had come along and our little world was suddenly perfect.

Naturally, Cole continued to work, but he took more time off than normal to spend with his son. He said he never wanted to be that absent father who spent more time at work than with his kid. And what a father he was. I had wondered if this ex-playboy with a reputation the size of Texas would be able to wrap his head around having a family all of his own, but he sank into the role as though it was what he had been waiting for all along, as though his life had been building up to this moment.

"Our boy is amazing, isn't he?" I sighed, leaning back against my husband's hard body.

He nodded. "He really is." He reached down and touched one

of Thomas' bare feet gently. "I can't believe he's going to be six months old tomorrow."

"Me neither," I shook my head. "It's amazing. It goes so fast."

"Yeah, it goes fast." He nuzzled into me again. "But maybe we could slow it down a little?"

"What do you mean?" I giggled, even though I knew precisely what he had in mind. He brushed his mouth over my neck playfully, sending a shiver down my spine.

We hadn't had a lot of time to indulge in just being a married couple before the baby came along, but he had taken a stand when Thomas arrived. He made sure we always had house-keepers and childcare. Everything we could want to keep the house running smoothly. Making time for me and him. Making time for him to romance me. Never before had I been in a relationship with a man who made me feel so valued, important, and vital to his life.

"Bedroom," he purred in my ear. "Now. Before he wakes up."

"But what if he—"

Before I could get the protest out, he scooped me into his arms and carried me out of the room. I looked over his shoulder to make sure we hadn't woken our son, but he was still sleeping peacefully, a little strand of brown hair laying over his forehead.

"Sir, sir, where are you taking me?" I demanded playfully.

"To make the most of the time we actually have together." He headed to the bedroom, kicking the door shut behind us.

"Oh, my goodness. You are such a caveman," I accused.

"Me?" he asked innocently while throwing me on the bed. Then he switched on the baby monitor because he knew I wouldn't be able to relax unless I knew Thomas was okay.

"Come here." I reached for my husband and pulled him down on top of me. Whoever had said that sex got boring after you were married just had no idea. If anything, things had gotten better between us since I knew he was completely committed to me, and wasn't looking anywhere else for his kicks. I'd felt my inhibitions lift, and we had indulged in things I never even imagined myself capable of before.

Yeah, even that.

And that.

For now, I knew I wanted nothing more than a good old-fashioned roll in the hay with my husband. He seemed more than willing to give that to me. Pushing my hands above my head and holding them down against the bed for a moment, he kissed me and I wriggled happily beneath him. Man, did he feel good. The weight of him, his heat, his strength.

"Hmm," he groaned, burying his nose in my neck and inhaling me as if I was some kind of heady perfume. "I think I know exactly what I want to do to you," he murmured. Then he was kissing down my chin, over my neck, his hands between my legs as he undid the zipper on the loose mom-jeans I'd slipped on that morning.

I wriggled on the bed as his mouth moved hungrily all over my skin. He pushed up the bottom of my shirt so he could kiss along my stomach. He knew that spot by now, the one just below my navel that made my head spin and he lingered there for a long, long time while I writhed and moaned, before he moved on.

Moved down.

He slid my jeans down over my hips, then hooked his fingers around my panties and pulled them off.

I kicked them to the floor below.

Cole then slipped back up between my legs, sinking his fingers deep into my thighs and letting out a long groan as he did so. "Man, I've missed having you like this," he growled softly, his voice laced with as much need as it had been the very first time we were together.

In fact, this reminded me of that, when he had touched me as though he never wanted to stop. Back then, I had wondered if this was how it was for every woman he slept with, but he had since dissuaded me of that idea, promising me it had been just as new for him as it had been for me.

He lowered his mouth to my pussy, stroking up my slit in one long stroke with his flattened tongue.

I groaned and arched my back from the bed. Reaching down, I gripped his silky hair to hold him in place. We didn't get much of a chance to do this these days, and I was so on-edge from all this wanting and waiting…. I was almost ready to go right then and there.

"Mmm," he moaned softly as he traced his tongue around my clit.

I pressed my feet into the bed, using the leverage to grind myself against his mouth. I was shameless now, not bothering to play coy, wanting nothing more than to feel his mouth on every part of me. He obliged, sucking my entire folds into his mouth, then tracing his tongue around my entrance before raising back up once more to focus his attention on my clit once more. He sealed his lips around me and sucked this time, with more purpose, the pressure tingling through every part of my body.

He moved his fingers between my legs with his other hand tucked under my ass, pulling me on to him greedily, like he couldn't get enough of me, and pushed his fingers into my pussy. And as soon as he entered me, I knew what I needed from him. But I figured, since he was so keen, I might as well let him indulge in tasting me for a little while. You know, for his sake.

"Fuck," I gasped as the mesh of sensation began to take me over. I loved this feeling, loved feeling lost to how good he was, how badly he wanted me and needed to taste me. His tongue moved slow and steady, the pressure constant and firm, his fingers not fucking me but feeling me, every inch of me, from the inside out. My hips were rising from the bed of their own accord and he was having to fight to keep me in place, but he was doing it, holding me there, his mouth on my pussy, until finally, finally...

I swallowed the cry, not wanting to wake up Thomas across the hall. Once you're a mother, you're a mother forever. Instead, the orgasm escaped me in endless tremors. They rocked me from top to toe, my body aching with the release, as he continued his movements against my clit, pushing me further and further until I felt as though I might pass out on the spot.

"Enough, enough," I groaned, reaching down and pushing his head away from my mound.

177

He looked up at me, a grin on his face, his mouth glistening with my wetness, and moved back on top of me. "My turn," he said, planting a kiss on my lips so I could taste myself on him.

"Yes, please," I breathed.

He unzipped his pants and pulled off his shirt before he shifted back on top of me. He had that look his eyes, the one he'd hit me with when I was walking up the aisle at our wedding, something between amazement and pride, as though he could hardly wrap his head around the fact, I was really his—that I always would be.

I arched my hips from the bed and he pressed the head of his erection against my slit, rubbing himself around my entrance a couple of times to tease me. We had long since disposed of the condoms. They didn't work for us anyway. I craved him deep and raw inside me every time we fucked now. The closeness was indescribable, impossible to recreate any other way. "Go on. Get inside me," I ordered impatiently. He liked it when I took control. I suppose he still wasn't used to being with someone who spoke their mind the way I did, and I was more than happy to indulge.

He grinned and thrust into me in one smooth motion, burying himself deep inside me.

I felt a surge of emotion when I remembered that this was how we had made our beautiful son together. I wrapped my arms around him and arched my back, letting him push in deeper. Then I lost myself to how amazing it felt to have my husband fuck me.

I wasn't sure how long we were making love like that, but it felt as though it spanned on forever, the way it always did with him. As though the world had slipped away, and all that was left was us. Fucking. I wrapped my legs around him and he held me tight in his arms, going hard, deep and slow, like he was savoring every moment.

Soon enough, I felt my second orgasm growing, my pussy tensing around him as he moved his hands over my waist, my thighs, and my ass. I buried my face in his shoulder as it hit me, giving myself over to the sweet bliss of his body and mine together.

"Fuck," he groaned in my ear as he reached his own release, stilling inside me as his own pleasure flooded through him.

I turned my face to his and kissed him deeply, pushing my tongue into his mouth, connecting on a deeper level, and extending the moment the only way I knew how.

Finally, we unwrapped ourselves from one another, and he flopped down on the bed next to me. Just as I caught my breath, I heard Thomas fidgeting and snuffling in sleep through the baby monitor.

"Let me get that," I muttered, pushing myself off the bed and stretching.

Before I could so much as get to my feet, Cole was upright and dressing quickly. "You stay right there. I'm going to take care of this."

"Well, no complaints here," I replied.

He moved towards me one last time and planted a kiss on my lips. "That was amazing."

"You're amazing," I blurted out with happy tears in my eyes, all soppy after our encounter.

"I'll be back in a minute." Cole grinned and headed towards the nursery to take care of our son.

I flopped back on the bed, listening to him talking to Thomas through the baby monitor, his deep voice cooing to his son and wondered if life could ever get any better than this.

The End

COMING SOON...

PRETEND FOR ME

Blurb

Willow

I never wanted to go to that party in the first place. I mean, what would an ordinary girl like me do amongst the crème de la crème of society? I'd rather have curled up with a good book at home, but my best friend was determined to go. She wanted us to dress up like Cinderella and pretend that we belonged at that party

I'll admit, she made me look good, better than I had ever expected. But surely not good enough to catch the eye of Kane Adams, one of the most eligible billionaires in the world.

And yet the ruggedly handsome hunk not only approached me, but told me he needed someone to pretend to be his wife and I was the perfect woman for the job. I nearly died when he mentioned the financial gain I would make, but once I'd got over the shock I had to admit I was in no position to turn down that once in a lifetime offer. Anyway, it wasn't like my life was filled with excitement as a waitress.

So I said sure I could pretend to be his wife. The problem came after we got married. When he accidentally crushed his lips against mine...and I accidentally melted in his arms.

Hmmm...obviously I didn't think this one through.

Willow

"The most amazing thing happened to me today," Loraine declared as she burst through the front door of our tiny apartment.

I lowered the book I was reading. "What?"

"You WILL never believe what I've got in my hand," she shouted, dancing the rumba, and waving a black card in her hand. Her eyes were shining like two very green buttons.

I looked at her expectantly. Unlike me Lorraine was an extremely dramatic person. She had what one would call a big personality. She was always the live wire at any party. The one that hit the dance floor first and the last to leave it. She was also my best friend and the only person in the world I trusted.

I was born a heroin baby, no father, no mother, and suffering withdrawal symptoms. It was in my records that a nurse called Miriam sat for hours in front of my incubator stroking me through the holes in the incubator. I still wonder about her because after her I knew no love throughout my childhood. Just foster families, five to be exact, who took care of me in exchange for money. I guess I have to count myself lucky since I was never beaten or sexually abused. I was just ignored.

I couldn't blame them I was a mousy, bespectacled and quiet child.

My life was dull and loveless and the only pleasure I found was from reading. At first fairy tales and books about child detectives, then when I was thirteen I read my first romance book. That was it. I was hooked. Within those pages I slipped into another wonderful world where gorgeous Alpha men saw beauty in ordinary gray girls like me, and fell in love with them. I spent hours and hours absorbed in that delightful fantasy world.

Lorraine had stopped dancing so I put my book on my lap and gave her my full attention.

"What is it?" I asked mildly.

"What is it?" she demanded. "That's your reaction to me saying the most amazing thing had happened to me?"

I hid a smile at her annoyance. "All right. Tell me what is this amazing thing that has happened to you."

She rushed to the sofa and held the card in front of me. I took it and glanced at it. The card was thick and black the writing was embossed in gold. It seemed to be an invitation to a party, and I honestly could not for the life of me imagine how it could be classed as amazing.

"Well?" she prompted.

I looked up at her shrugged. "What is it? It just looks like an invitation to a party to me."

"Just an invitation to a party?" she screeched. "Have you never heard of the Ambonnay gala?"

I shook my head. "No. Should I have?"

She sank down next to me. "Guuuurl, it is time you got your cute little button nose out of those romance books of yours and lived a little. The Zeitgeist party is just the most important party in the world. I mean, people kill to go to these events."

I made a disbelieving face.

"I'm serious. This party is where the crème de la crème of society go. It is packed with the 0.1%. Last year Kim Kardashian tried to go. She hinted about it on Twitter, but in the end she couldn't get an invite so she had to pretend she didn't want to go because she was too busy bickering with her mother, one of her sisters, husband, or kids."

I gave the card back to her. "Right. So how did you get your hot paws on this then."

"That is the second most amazing part of my story. It was purely by chance. It could so easily have gone to someone else."

I smiled and sat back in anticipation of a good story.

She gave a grin and put the card on the table. "Bella was sick today so Matthew asked me to take over her section. At about eight a couple came in. The woman was one of those Hollywood actress types. She was wearing a divine red dress and her face was so done up you couldn't tell if she was in her late twenties or seventies. The guy though, was very handsome and young, maybe in his early twenties. I got the impression he was subservient to her, like he was her body-guard or masseur. Even so they made a good-looking couple so I showed them to table nine."

I nodded. That's what I would have done too if I had been working in the restaurant tonight. Table nine was where we put the beautiful people because it was right in the middle and everybody got to see them. It made the restaurant look glamorous.

"The whole time they kept holding hands and looking deep into each other's eyes. They were so madly in love the woman hardly touched her meal. Then over dessert the man gets on his knees in front of the whole restaurant and proposes to her."

My eyebrows rose in surprise. All the time I had been working in that restaurant nothing like that had ever happened.

"She was so happy she cried. Well, she didn't really cry, but she dabbed away some imaginary tears from her perfectly made-up eyes."

She paid the bill, and when I brought her receipt back, she gave me this invitation. She said, she was leaving her husband so she no longer needed it. I mean, can you believe it? I was just at the right place at the right time."

I frowned. "So you're going to go to this party?"

"We are," she said with a grin.

"No, no, count me out. I would be like a fish out of water in those kinds of environment."

"No, you won't. Just leave it to me. I'll take care of everything. I'll be your fairy godmother. I'll make you look so beautiful you'll be like Cinderella at the ball."

"Listen Loraine. I know you mean well and you think you are doing me a favor by taking me to this party, but I really don't want to go. Why don't you take Susan or even Bella. They would love it."

She frowned. "But I want you to go with me."

"I would be so awkward around all those celebrities and billionaires."

"No, you won't. You'll be with me. I promise I won't let you out of my sight. Come on, it will be such a great experience. It'll be something to tell our grandchildren."

I shook my head. "Thanks, but no thanks."

She sat back and stared at me. "Remember that time when you came down with the female version of man flu?"

I had pneumonia," I corrected dryly.

She waved her hand carelessly to show she had no interest in petty details. "I covered five shifts for you, which means I did not have a break for two whole weeks. When I said I didn't want you to pay me back, you said you would owe me one. Well, I'm calling in the favor now."

I gazed into her serious eyes. She really wanted me to go with her. Thoughts about our lives together flashed into my brain. How hard we worked just to cover our bills. Both us working every shift and Lorraine working as a cleaner in a swanky apartment two mornings a week. At least, I had my books to hide in. She had nothing. We were both orphans. This was Lorraine, my best friend. The person I cared about most in the whole world and I'd do everything in my power to make her happy. Going to a party where I would feel awkward and self-conscious all night would be nothing if it would make her happy.

I smiled at her. "Of course, I'll go with you. We'll be two Cinderellas at the ball."

As if she had been stung in the butt she launched into the air with a scream. Pulling me up by my wrists and laughing madly she dragged me along as she energetically did her happy dance.

"I got a good feeling about this. I promise, you won't regret saying yes," she gasped.

I probably will, but what the hell. If it made her happy I was good with it.

To be continued...

Pretend For Me will be available on the
20th of March

ALSO BY RIVER LAURENT